"Stephen, I thought we were in a tiny clearing. How did those three trees get so close to us?"

Mandrakes!

There was not even time to lift a weapon. It was hand to hand, but the Mandrakes had many hands. Their tendrils lashed your eyes and clogged your ears. Stephen was by far the strongest boy in the village, but it would take a Samson to fight these moving trees, and he began to hope that he had not led John and Miriam to their deaths.

Suddenly, he was flung to the ground by the lash of a tentacle. There was a heavy weight on his chest . . . choking tendrils in his mouth and nose . . . he could not breathe. . . .

THE TOURNAMENT OF THORNS

by

THOMAS BURNETT SWANN

ace books
A Division of Grosset & Dunlap, Inc.
1120 Avenue of the Americas
New York, New York 10036

THE TOURNAMENT OF THORNS

An ACE Book

Dedication:
To Grover, His Book

First ACE printing: July 1976

Printed in U.S.A.

Another ACE Book
by Thomas Burnett Swann
you will enjoy:

LADY OF THE BEES

ACKNOWLEDGMENTS

I wish to express with gratitude a large debt to *A History of Everyday Things in England: 1066-1499* by Marjorie and C. H. B. Quennell and *The Crusades* by Henry Treece. With one exception, the songs quoted in my story are modernized versions of anonymous Old and Middle English lyrics. The exception is original, my Unicorn Song, reprinted with the permission of The Wings Press.

T.B.S.

Part One: Stephen

I

I am thirty-five, a woman of middle years, and yet in this time of pox and plague, of early death and the dying of beauty before the body dies, it is said that I am still as beautiful as a Byzantine Madonna, poised in the heaven of a gold mosaic and wearing sorrow like a robe of petals. But sorrow is not a gown. It is a nakedness to the searching eye, to the magpie-tongued who love to pry out grief. . . . She grieves too long. . . . The Manor demands an heir. . . . Who will defend us from the encroaching forest, the thieves and the Mandrake People?

It was eleven years ago, in the year 1202 of Our

Lord, that my husband's comrade-in-arms, Edmund-the-Wolf, rode to me with the news of my husband's death and, for the grieving widow, the riches captured before he had died in battle. Captured? Pillaged, I should say, in the sack of Constantinople. You see, it is a time when men are boys, rapacious and cruel, as ready to kill a Jew, a Hungarian, or a Greek as an Infidel; when men are happy so long as they wield a sword and claim to serve God — Crusading it is called. A time when boys who have not yet grown to their fathers' pride are the only true men.

And yet I loved my husband, a red-haired Norman, gay as the men of the South, and not like most of our stern northern people. I loved him for his gaiety, his hair the color of Roman bricks, and because he left me a son.

But the Crusader's code, like an evil demon of pox, also possesses children. In France and Germany, only last year, Stephen proclaimed his message from Christ, Nicholas piped his irresistible flute, and the children yearned to them as tides to the moon, flowing in a sea of white immaculate robes toward the shores of that greater sea, the Mediterranean.

Little of the madness crossed to England. Perhaps our children are not inclined to visions, perhaps they prefer the hunt to the drafty halls of a church and talks with God. But the madness, missing the thousands, somehow touched my son. He rode to London, astride his roan palfrey and dressed in a jerkin of sheepskin dyed to the yellow of gorse, with a leather belt at his waist and a fawn-colored pouch ajingle with new-minted pennies. Ready to board a ship for Marseilles and join Stephen! But Stephen and most of his army were sold as slaves to the Infidels; Nicholas died of the plague before he reached the sea . . . and my son of fifteen summers, reaching London, stood on the banks of the Thames to choose what twin-castled ship would bear him across the channel, and fell to the blade of a cutpurse thrice his years. The Devil, I think, possessed the children, a jest to fling like a gauntlet in the teeth of God.

God is not blind, however. In less than a year, he sent me those other children struck with the same madness: John, a dark-haired Norman; Stephen, a Saxon named like the boy of France.

Poor, proud Stephen, how you mistrusted me! I only wished you well, I only wished you welfaring through the woods of your dream. Stephen who, long of coming, companioned by John, beloved by Miriam, came to me from the Mandrake lair, the haunts of the unicorn. . . .

"Come to the fair!"
They might have said "Holy Land!"

He had come for practical things, lentils to cook and wool to weave, and a rare extravagance, a pinch of nard for his mother, the prettiest woman from here to London Town. But how could he bargain before he had looked and savored, reveled in freedom, shaken his golden mane and caught the eye of a girl?

"Rhubarb and sparrowgrass!"

"Silks from Jerusalem!"

"Blades from Damascus, sharper than Infidel swords!"

Ah, to be rich like Ralph, the Falcon, lord of the castle! Tent-like stalls, bright as daffodils, ranged in the wide, protective shadow of the keep. Merchants had brought their wares from Chichester Town; returning Crusaders brought spoils from the Holy Land. But Stephen, big, ruddy, blond, handsome enough to bedazzle a Saracen princess, was a simple villein's son. His longest journey had been to hunt in the woods, and the girls he had loved must be dreamed into princesses.

"Stephen." The voice was small but firm; the speaker was John, son to Ralph, the Falcon. He stood in the door to the keep and smiled a shy, tentative smile.

If Stephen had been a conquering Norman instead of a conquered Saxon, he might have become John's friend. But he was the son of a serf, and his father's ears had been cropped when a lamb he had sent to his lord, John's father, had caused that redoubtable baron a gripe in the stomach and frequent climbs to the *garderobe* atop his stairs.

"John! Aren't you coming to the fair?"

"My father is punishing me. I missed a pheasant at twenty paces. He says I'm clumsy as a . . ."

"Villein?"

"Yes. I didn't mean to tell you, though. *You* would never have missed."

"And neither would you, if someone taught you to aim. I could teach you but —"

"Enjoy the fair," said the child, vanishing into the keep. Evaporating, thought Stephen. Priest, scholar, poet — he is not of this castle or town. Heaven would give him a home, or the Valley of the Unicorns.

Still, he had come to the fair and not to see John. He had looked and now he must spend. Who could advise him about the proper price of things? Silver-tongued charlatans bleached the bones of a dog and sold them for those of a saint; extracted the juice of violets and called it nard. He must find a friend. There, in the midst of the crowd — Timothy and Leah. Old as the keep, they looked, both using canes, but friends of his parents and wise against liar and thief. A fat, warty man, Michael by name, was berating their little girl. His wife, Rachel, nodded in approbation.

"Plumper than suits a villein's child. And rosier too. Why, England is one big pauper since Richard's day!" Then, to the child's father, "Plump and rosy, my friend, and you a poor, bent man. I think you've a Mandrake in your family. Ever give her the test?"

Timothy's eyes belied the calm of his voice. His words were low and precise. "Everyone knows she came from the Fairy Folk when we lost our Ann to the Plague. Kept my wife from losin' her mind, she

7

did. 'Sides, she's much too biddable to be a Mandrake babe. Most o' their young are vain little critters. Always the lookin' glass, the latest scent from Paris."

"Rebecca is not a Mandrake." Stephen had come for help; he had come *to* help. He spoke with anger to hide his ignorance.

"What do you know about Mandrakes, young fellow?"

"More than a mite," said Stephen, affecting the casual air of a priest or a scholar, secure in knowledge if not in years. "Came from the north, some say, when Richard went to the wars and took his knights. Dug their tunnels, planted seeds in the ground to grow their young. Multiplied till even the wolves were afraid."

"That all you know?"

"Sometimes pass their girls into human families. Not their boys. Look like vegetables from the start. The Stalking Trees, they're called."

"Smart young fellow, aren't you? But I can tell you more. Case right here in town when you were a babe. Woodcutter name o' Thomas found a girl on his hearth. Wife said to keep her. Thought her a fairy changeling. Afraid *not* to keep her. Fairies are mean in the Heath. Fierce as a Manticore. Girl grew ripe and rosy like an apple. Parents sickened and pined and finally died. Girl was alone in the house. Skin turned whiter than chalk. Grew a beard like a man, and green at that. Ate all the time or sat in front of a mirror and looked and wept. A Mandrake, that's

8

what she was. Had to kill her, we did. Burned her at the stake."

Stephen stifled a shudder and fixed his features into a look of scorn.

"Now we test 'em, the ones in doubt. Stick an arm or a leg until they bleed. Blood thick as resin? Greenish instead of red? Cut off her head and quarter the part that's left. The best aphrodisiac anyone ever could buy. The Scriptures tell you that. Saw one here at the fair, sliced and dried in the sun."

"And another one still on its feet," said Rachel. She was the kind of woman Michael deserved for a wife — a woman who preferred brambles to roses. "Why, Rebecca spends half her time with my little Sarah and looks twice as plump. And Sarah ailing so's we left her at home today."

"I say put your child to the test," pronounced Michael. He brandished a Saracen blade, a scimitar more than a knife, its hilt emblazoned with a crescent moon. By now the argument had attracted a crowd. A three-legged pig grunted in vain for attention. Fine round cheeses attracted mongrels instead of men.

"A Mandrake is it, you say?"

"Sure as God kicked Lucifer out of Heaven."

"Burn her, what else?"

"Quarter her, dunderhead. Worth a Richard's ransom in aphrodisiacs."

They looked at the child, they listened and pointed and gestured, called to their friends, repeated the cause of the fray.

Stephen was not an orator, but neither was he a coward. "Cut that child and you'll think the Saracens got you."

Michael scowled and peered quizzically at his youthful challenger: the gold of him, gold like a halo atop his head; the height and weight of him, like Jacob's angel.

"Who's this talking? The biggest womanizer in town! Waitin' till little Rebecca's old enough for the hay?"

Stephen lifted him by the nape of his neck and held him above the ground. "When she's old enough for the hay, she'll wed a knight and I'll be in Jerusalem. I'm here now, though. You aren't."

He not only dropped the man, warts, weight, and all, he flung him onto his face, and the fickle crowd, amused if not glutted, cackled with laughter which sounded uncannily like a flock of crows assaulting a barley field.

"Come here, Rebecca," smiled Stephen. "That wicked old bogey won't bother you anymore."

Rebecca was used to caresses instead of curses. Four years old, a wonder of red-gold hair and rosebud lips, she ran into Stephen's arms.

"What about a game of Hoodman Blind?" he asked.

"That can wait," said her grateful father. "First you must make your purchases and then you shall sup with us. That is to say, if you like what we have in our basket."

"But have you enough?" Stephen had thought to

miss his lunch and save his pennies for nard.

"Always for a friend. Now what do you need? Nard, you say? I have a friend you can trust. . . ."

"Shall we eat outside the walls?" asked Leah, a woman of eloquent silences. Words, she felt, should only be used for a purpose, never to pass the time. "The crowd is making Rebecca nervous."

The three-legged pig had inspired a traveling player to sing a ballad with unrepeatable rhymes. A mirror of glass, a rarity from the Holy Land, had attracted a swarm of ladies accustomed to bronze.

"It's safe, I think. Ralph, for once, is at peace with his neighbors. The Mandrakes keep their distance from the castle. Wolves only come at night."

Beyond the keep, beyond the moat which had shrunk to a ring of mud, they spread their simple fare on the daffadowndilly grass. Simple? For Stephen a feast! A pie with an amber crust; ewes' milk cheese; gingerbread soaked in honey; and a hogshead of foaming beer.

"And now for a nap," said Timothy. " 'Eat meat, sleep deep.' That's what Richard said after every battle."

Luxury upon luxury! A fair, a feast, and a nap in the middle of the day. Stephen rested his head on a mound of daffodils, and his waking dreams became a part of his sleep. He was a Saxon king like his great-great-grandfather, instead of a Saxon villein under a Norman overlord. He battled Mandrakes and rescued nubile princesses. Then, like every man who some-

11

times prefers the company of his own sex, he gathered his comrades and dogs into an army and marched to Jerusalem.

Curiously, he awoke to a kiss. Rebecca was kneeling beside him and pressing her lips against his cheek.

"Big Stephen, will you always look after me?"

"Always," he promised. He could never deny a child or a pretty girl; a dog or a friend. "Now I must start for home. I've quite a walk, you know. Stay with your parents, Rebecca. Let them sleep. They were very tired."

He sat up with tremendous effort; he tried to rise. A bewildering lassitude pervaded his sturdy frame, like the aftermath of a fever. He touched a hand to his cheek and remembered a piece of lore from one of his friends, who had traveled to London with a band of knights and returned, to Stephen at least, a man of the world: "It is only vampires from Hungary who pierce the skin. The Mandrakes are much more subtle. They draw your blood through the pores, and sometimes they mean to kiss instead of vampirize. The girls who have passed, I mean. Their forest brothers devour instead of draw."

"Stephen," she said. "I'm never afraid with you." Roses could envy her lips; her voice was a windchime in an apple tree.

"Can't get up, can you?" It was Michael, of course. "You still think we shouldn't put her to the test?"

"What . . . what do you mean?" He had to wrench the words from his sluggish tongue.

12

The fair had begun to disperse, the sun was about to be swallowed by oaks and sycamore, green and august reminders that England was a great kingdom but also a great wilderness. People meandered past him with curious looks: women in hooded gowns; men in knee-length tunics and long stockings or chausses; colorless women, old before their time; shuffling men, patient with poverty.

"Look," cried Michael to the passersby. "Here is your Stephen now. Ready to wrestle a bear, eh, boy?"

Stephen lurched to his feet, fell to his knees, then rose with one supreme effort to confront a grin and a pair of porcine eyes.

"Looks like the bear won," suggested Rachel, her voice like the tearing of silk in a bramble bush.

Michael, sure of his evidence, snatched Rebecca into his bloated arms.

"No," said Stephen, trying to shout. He swayed in his tracks. He could not take a step.

Gloatingly, almost leisurely, Michael performed the test with his Saracen blade. Rebecca looked bewildered instead of hurt; she did not utter a cry at the bite of steel.

The blade was covered with viscous, greenish blood.

Michael bristled with triumph.

"Burn her!" shouted his wife.

Timothy and Leah awoke at last from their sleep. They saw; they screamed; they struggled against their friends.

"Burn her, burn her, burn her!" The cries resounded

13

from forest to keep, from keep to forest, multiplied into one huge cacophony of hatred and fear.

With a deft and confident blow, Michael severed her head. Her veins and arteries looked like roots.

"Easier this way. 'Sides, who'll buy ashes."

Stephen fell to the ground with a violent cramp.

The sun had set, a copper shield eclipsed by trees. His father had come from the barley fields; his mother was waiting anxiously at the door.

"I heard some wolves in the night," she said. "I was worried about you, Son. It's such a ways to the castle. All those trees and sedges—Stephen, why are you crying?"

"I bought the lentils and wool. And here—did you ever see such a handsome vial? The nard's inside."

"In faith, it's amber. But something has happened to you, Son. I never saw you so pale."

Only her eyes showed years and toil. A baron's wife would have envied the rest of her, the grace of her body, the fine small bones of her face. She might have stepped from a lordly wooden hall in the time before the Conquest. In truth, she claimed descent from a Saxon king. She always smelled of clover or bergamot, and once, it was said, she had met a unicorn in the forest and asked him the secret of immortality. Stephen called her his Lady of Daffodils, because of her yellow hair. Her vanity was never to wear a hood.

Stephen embraced her with a rough, urgent tenderness.

14

"A Mandrake," he said. "At the fair—"

"How horrible."

"No, Mother, you don't understand. It was little Rebecca."

He recounted the tale in a dull, listless voice. He would soon be a man; it would not become him to cry.

His mother brushed a tear with the edge of her sleeve. "My poor Stephen. You have seen an execution instead of a fair."

"Why couldn't they have put her in the forest for her own people to find?"

"To grow and mate and give birth to another Mandrake?" his father asked. He always approached on silent feet, as if he had come to fear his own footsteps. "God knows—or should by now—with wolves, robbers, and contentious barons, we have enough to dread. Be glad the beheading was quick. She never felt a thing. I'm proud of the way you stood her champion, though, till the truth was known."

His father had been the kindest and comeliest boy in the village. Now, his cropped ears made his head look long and thin, like the hilt of a sword, and he was scarred and leathery like an old saddle from toiling at many tasks in many weathers. But Stephen loved him next to his mother.

"I must feed Bucephalus," Stephen said. His dog was a cur and not a thoroughbred; his noble name had belonged to the favorite horse of Alexander the Great, dreamer, conqueror, and, to Stephen at least, foremost among the saints. Under a lean-to behind the house, he took the dog in his arms. Touch to Stephen was more meaningful than words and, touching Bucephalus, he tried to forget Rebecca. *I will think of the gentlest person I know besides my mother. I will think of John.*

It never occurred to him that John and the Mandrakes and also a grave-eyed, fierce-horned Unicorn would soon become a part of his life as well as his dreams and nightmares.

II

    To Stephen, the fair had become Rebecca instead
of John, Leah, and Timothy; hemlock instead of nard.
But who had time to brood with a field to work? The
local villeins worked the three-field system—one to
grow wheat, one to grow oats, one to lie fallow until
another year. He and his father had toiled a tedious
day on the five acres they held in the name of Ralph,
the Falcon, who held them in the name of John, the

Weakling, brother to the late and beloved Richard, the Lion-Heart.

It was a day for sowing oats. It was Stephen's duty to follow his father through the fields and scatter the greedy crows with well-aimed stones from his sling. Beyond a hillock, piebald cattle grazed in the common land; undulant vineyards, promising grapes as big as chestnuts, lured the bee and the wasp and seemed to borrow their hum. Tranquility lay like a mantle across the land, but a cerement, not a cloak. For Ralph, the Falcon, was a harsh accountant.

"Pay me with produce or pay me with lives," he liked to boast. "A third of your grapes and grain; chicken and calves and pigs in any number I name; and wool from the looms in the huts I so graciously lend to you. Am I not a generous man?"

Watching his father, Stephen sighed and thought, How many sowings until I am broken like you? Gone, the gold of my hair, the spring in my step. Gone, the girls who flutter and coo like doves when I give them the eye. Day follows day; seedtime, weeding, harvest; only a different girl to mark a different year. Christ's Wounds! Will I never wield a sword instead of a hoe? Fight in the Holy Land for the glory of God and the rout of the Infidel? Why, in France another Stephen, almost my age, is marching to join Nicholas in the port of Outre-Mer! I will be splitting firewood while they are battling Saracens. . . .

"Stephen," his father called. "The crows are eating the grain."

Stephen quickly dispersed them with his sling. "Father, forgive me. What can I say?"

"No need, Son. If we couldn't dream! . . . It's not everyone who can sail to Jerusalem. Some of us have to build it in our minds. Go to your mother now. Pick her a wreath of daffodils. Hers is a harder lot than yours or mine. She must work alone, and you know how she likes a house which is brimful of guests."

"It doesn't take many for ours to brim."

"Stephen, so bitter of late? Has a girl said no to you?"

"Yes," said Stephen, "but that's not the reason, Father. Time, we think, is our friend. He brings us harvest, he brings us babies and puppies. But lately, it seems, he's taken more than he's brought."

"Pick those flowers. Cheer your mother and she will cheer us both."

It was a house of timbers daubed with clay; a humble house—one room, one window, one gabled loft; a table, a bench, a set of earthenware mugs, a wooden chest for linen and wool and cloves. (Humble? "Fit for a fairy queen!" his mother would say. "A man must duck his head to enter the door, but once he enters he will want to bide. Did ever a fairy keep an ungracious house?")

"Stephen, you've brought me daffodils!"

"It was Father's thought."

"Yours too, I expect. See, I shall set them here in the window seat to catch the sun."

"I meant you to make a garland for your hair."

19

"Would that please you best? You make the garland then. I am a unicorn, sweet from the piney woods, and you, my dear—"

"You can't be a unicorn," he laughed. "Or how can I garland you? They only like virgins. *Female* virgins, I mean. Possibly a priest would do."

"Well, then, since you are neither a priest nor a female virgin, you shall have to be just my son, of whom I am very proud, and I am your mother, Joanna, a villein's wife. What do we need with a unicorn?"

"Father was right," he said.

"How do you mean?"

"That you would cheer me up."

"But you have cheered *me*."

"It's the same thing. Now I must chop some wood."

'We've enough for the supper fire. Rest in the windowseat. Boys weren't meant to work from dawn to dusk and sleep the whole night through. There must be a time for sport." (By the Holy Rood, did she know about his girls?)

She whispered a kiss across his cheek. "Every boy is born with an inclination, I think—a gift or a curse —from God, the fairies, or a patron saint—for song and for merriment. But poverty gets in the way. What do you do? Knock him flat on his back. Strong, is he? Knee him in the groin. Crafty and cruel? Pray to Alexander, your warrior saint. What I am trying to tell you, Son, is this. Your life should be more than a tournament of thorns. You ought to find roses too. I think you were meant to be a merry boy. Why don't you go to the village before it gets dark and try your hand at a game of knucklebones? Lucky Stephen, that's what I've heard you called."

"I would rather stay here with you." He paused and deliberated and, not for the first time, asked a question which greatly puzzled him. "When you were a girl, did you really meet a unicorn?"

"That must be my secret," she smiled. "You've asked me often enough, and often enough I've asked you not to ask. If I did meet one, it wouldn't be right to tell, now, would it?"

"Some people meet them and tell."

"Some people *say* they meet them. Certain young girls I know whose qualifications are doubtful, to say the least."

"But you can tell me what they're like. You've read about them in a bestiary." Both of his parents could read a codex as well as the castle chaplain, quote from the Scriptures, or study the lives of the saints. They had not, however, persuaded their son to read. ("Study by candlelight? Why, the price of a candle can buy a loaf of bread!")

"To the monks and the friars they symbolize the soul," she said. "Their horns point eternally toward the heavens. Yet here on Earth, like all good folk, they have their mortal foes."

"The Mandrakes."

"Who symbolize lust and sloth." The setting sun had touched her hair to gold. The gown she wore, homespun but bluer than blue-bell blossoms, en-

21

folded her body in a softness of wool.

"Don't stop, Mother."

"But I've told you these things a hundred times, my dear."

"Tell me about the Tradition."

She shrugged and smiled. "How can I mend your tunic and talk about unicorns? I've clothes to wash, lye to make from last night's ashes. You're making a lazybones out of your mother. You tell *me* for a change."

"When good folk die, they don't always go to Heaven. Not right away, at least." (He envisioned a Heaven of angels wearing haloes and playing harps. He preferred Jerusalem. Wings were practical, haloes becoming, but harps! Why not rebecs and kettle-drums?) "If they like, they can linger on Earth as unicorns to protect the ones they love. There now. It's your turn again. How does a unicorn look? He surely isn't a deer who's lost a horn."

"Their fur is as gossamer as a butterfly's wing. Their horns are mother-of-pearl. And when they run they can overtake the wind!"

"I've never seen one," he sighed. "Not even a glimpse. I've taken the swine to root in the forest. I've cut firewood. Once I walked all the way to Chichester to get you that camphor when you were sick. Wolves, deer, but never a unicorn."

She patted him gently on the head. "Boys like to hunt and carouse. It's part of their nature, part of their growing up, and the unicorns are shy."

"But if I could find a virgin to walk with me —"

"Then they might show themselves."

"Like the one you saw."

"Stephen, Stephen, would you want me to break a promise?" She paused at her loom and distance blued her eyes into bits of sky, as if she had glimpsed her own Jerusalem.

"Well, I would like to look for one in spite of my nature. Maybe he could lead me to the Holy Land."

"They would never lead you to war," she said. "Except against Mandrake Folk. And a good thing too. The Holy Land resisted the mighty Richard. What might it do to a boy?"

"He would have won except for his craven allies. All it takes is the right support, and Jerusalem will fall in our hands like a ripe fig."

"The fig is protected by many bees, I fear. And who will you get for allies? The children of France and Germany?"

"And England. If only we had a unicorn for luck."

"Here. You can churn the milk. We've talked enough about unicorns."

It was night. The moon was a manor house of rounded ivory, and Miriam, like a princess of Navarre, had walked to Earth on a bridge of curving light.

"Stephen," she smiled, extending a hand which instantly broke his dream, for she, like him, was a villein's child and her hand was red from toil.

23

"The leaves make a *lovely* couch," he said. Only princesses need be virgins.

"Dearest Stephen," she smiled. "You want a bumptious lass. I have told you before that I am much too grave for you."

"That is for me to decide. I like some grav—gravity in a girl." Was that the word? "I never said you ought to be bumptious. Just willing."

"Boys and girls can be friends without making love."

"I have all the friends I need. I've a dog, and William in the village, and Antony, the gatekeeper—"

"I haven't, Stephen. Be *my* friend." The moonlight haloed her brown Norman hair and made of her eyes a wounding wonderment.

"All right then," he sighed. "I'll be your friend. But it isn't the same at all."

"It's not the same, but that doesn't mean it's less. Different, that's all. You asked me to join you when you sail for Jerusalem. I *must* be a friend, a comrade-in-arms. A light-o-love would distract you from the wars."

"That's true," he confessed. "The Crusades are first, or should be, with every Christian. After the crops are in, I think we should walk to London and there take ship to France." It was not a practical dream; he could never forsake an aging father and a burdened mother. Still, he could plan with Miriam under their mossy tree, their Merlin tree, which looked like a wizard with an untrimmed beard.

"But we need a guide," she said.

"A unicorn."

"Your mother saw one, didn't she?"

"She won't tell me for sure."

"Can't tell you. But you've noticed how young she looks? How she never seems to age? Why, she must be upwards of forty, and most of her friends are bent old women. But she has a face as pure as that moon above our tree, and her hands are soft and white instead of red like mine."

"Well, she won't help us, and that's that. We shall just have to find our own. The trouble is, when you look for a unicorn, you may find a Mandrake. And after Rebecca's death! Why, they must be out for blood. More than usual, I mean."

"You don't exactly find them, I understand. They happen upon you and smother or choke you to death."

"It works both ways. Michael happened on little Rebecca. Sometimes I wonder what's the answer."

"Sometimes there's only a question. I have to go now, Stephen. It's late and my parents will worry."

"Because you're here with me."

"A bit," she confessed. "Your habits are rather familiar."

"Sleep is a little death. I would rather talk."

"Tomorrow then." She brushed his cheek with a quick, sisterly kiss. Would he never graduate to her mouth?

"Good night, Miriam. Moon Girl." (In spite of her hands.)

They returned their separate ways to their cottages. Not that Miriam feared the gossips' tongue. She always said, "I mean to behave, and if people think I'm bad, they are to blame, not me." But he knew the viciousness of the womenfolk, and he knew his reputation with the girls.

As he neared his cottage, he heard Bucephalus bark. The dog was chained at night because he liked to forage among the neighbor's chickens, thinking, no doubt, to provide his master with a change of diet; meat instead of cheese.

Stephen hastened his steps to the lean-to behind his house and caught the dog in his arms. Bucephalus lacked an ear from a fight with a wolf. His fur had the look of mud. The mudpie dog, he was called by Stephen's friends. His head was large, his tail was long, and a good deal of animal joined the two extremities.

"There, old fellow. Lonesome, are you? So am I. We could both use some company."

Bucephalus' bark became a frenzied yelp.

"Hush, hush, old man! Do you want to wake the house? No, you want to show me something, don't you?"

A cutpurse, a leper, a wolf. . . . The forest was rife with such perils, the castle a poor defense to scattered cottages and feeble cottagers. Quickly he loosened Bucephalus' chain.

Dog beside him, he stared through the door of his house. Unbarred for his return. Open to friends or strangers.

In the lanternless, moondusted room, he saw three figures, huddled, hunched, and white. Lepers, he thought. They have come to steal our food. Their garments hang upon them in tattered rags.

The men made a rush to escape. Their move released an odor as rank as a slimy bog; a cry like the howl of a wounded Manticore. Bucephalus reared in surprise like a skittish colt and knocked him to the ground. He saw three backs, stark in the light of the moon.

No, they were trunks, a horror of writhing tendrils and flailing limbs.

No, they were not even trees. They lacked the naturalness of trunk and limb. Distortions. Perversions. Trees mimicking men.

Mandrakes. . . .

"My mother," he whispered (to whom he did not know). "Her arm shouldn't hang like that. And the blood on Father's face — the moonlight makes it black."

"Hush, boy. You've seen enough for the night."

"We tried to stop them, Bucephalus and I. But first, you see, we had to look to my parents."

"And so you did."

"But now we can go to look for the —"

"Not in the dark. Not for Mandrakes. Here, drink this."

The potion was bitter and thick; it made him think

of the slime he had seen at the door. . . . It made him
cease to think. . . .

He climbed the stairs of consciousness, step by
step, a cripple without a cane . . . light at the top . . .
voices, many and harsh . . . Ralph, the Falcon.

"The house can go for firewood. It isn't fit for living. Too isolated. Last night proved that."

(*His coat is lined with fur. His shoes have leather
points and shiny copper buttons. . . .*)

"They must have come because of that child who
was killed at the fair. Rebecca, was that her name?
Chose the furthest cottage."

"And the boy?" The Baron was flushed from drink,
foully odorous beneath his coat. "What's he good for?"

"He's good with animals."

"I need a new dog boy. He can tend my hounds.
The last boy fell asleep too often. I had to take steps."

"No," said Stephen weakly, fumbling after words.
"No, I don't like you. I don't want to tend your dogs.
I couldn't stand to see you kick them."

"When he's more coherent, bring him to the castle."
No doubt he was late for a hunt.

"Cry, Stephen, cry all you like. The others have
gone away." A tentative hand, a butterfly hand, ex-
tended to touch his arm. John!

"I cried too when my mother died."

"Did you, John?"

"Yes. But there was no one to hold. It made a difference."

"I haven't anyone either. Mother without any daffodils. And Father — they should have hidden his ears. He was always ashamed of them."

"There's me. To hold I mean. I'm good for that, at least. Or I could look for your dog. He wasn't hurt, you know."

"Could you?"

"Whatever you say, Stephen."

"Not now. You mustn't go just yet."

"Not even to find Bucephalus?"

"You know his name!"

"Oh, yes. I quite envied him. Because he had a friend for a master."

"Have I another friend?"

He felt the child's embrace like a sudden, subtle warmth, the peep of sun above his windowseat. It was hesitant, bodiless, almost, and bountiful beyond the riches of France or Rome.

"I know a healing spot," said John. "Here, give me your hand. You can't see to walk through all those tears."

The spot was the mossy turf beneath the Merlin tree.

"When my father has me bladed, I come here to rest. It's the only place I can sit. I've seen you here with a girl. Miriam, isn't it? The one with the face of a saint."

"We never saw you, John."

"I know. Until the fair, I thought you would *never* notice me. Then you smiled and spoke. That's why I came today. Stayed when the others left."

"I noticed you a long time ago, when your own mother died and you were a little boy. I wanted to bring you home for a bite of cheese and a nip of beer — that was all we had. But you were the Baron's son. I daren't speak a word."

"I understand. Father was drunk at the time. But if he had caught me with a villein's son — a Saxon at that! — I couldn't have sat for a year. I sleep in the great hall with the sons of the knights, and I'm supposed to be friends only with them, but I'm not friends with any of them. If he catches me now, I really don't think I care."

"Truly, John?"

"You promised to teach me how to aim a bow. Remember? And I can teach you about the things I learn from the chaplain. How many angels can dance on the head of a pin. The names of all the Devils in Hell."

"And unicorns?"

"I don't know much about unicorns. I think it's virgins they like, not boys."

"Never mind. You can get your chaplain to tell you about Mandrakes, and then tell me. I'm going after them. The ones who killed my parents."

"I don't blame you. Your mother was the prettiest lady in all the town. Everyone said she was. Joanna, the Lady of the Daffodils. When my mother died, she sent me a little wreath of violets."

"Did you cry when she died? For a long time, I mean?"

"For a solid week! And I didn't eat a thing. All I remember is that it always seemed to be raining. But it wasn't raining at all. It was the gray kind of way I looked at things. The way you see things now."

"And always will."

"No, Stephen. There are too many things to remember. Good things. After awhile, you learn to sift. Did you know that my mother liked a garland better than gold and jewels? She would wear a crown of marigolds to a festival, and my father would fume, 'Where are the rubies I stole from Hungary?' I expect your mother was much the same. Now I had better take you to the kennels. I'm afraid you'll have to sleep in the hay. You'll smell of dog and everybody will forget your name and call you the Dog Boy. Except me, of course."

"Can I bring Bucephalus to live with me there?"

"Oh, no, he's only a mongrel. Father breeds greyhounds."

"I guess he considers Saxons a kind of mongrel."

"I don't. Your blood is purer than mine, and I've always envied your yellow hair. Maybe you can give your dog to somebody in the village."

"And still slip off to see him at night!"

"I'll bribe the gatekeeper not to tell my father. If a dog gets sick, however, it's you who'll get the blame, and a good cuffing to boot."

"I don't care. I love them already."

"I knew you would. And something else. You'll live inside the walls. And I can come to see you every day when my father hunts."

There would be girls for Stephen, many of them. There would be friends among the village boys, many of them, and every dog who ever licked his hand.

But John was first.

Yes, even before Bucephalus.

III

He slept on a bed of straw in the loft above the
kennels, but he slept lightly, listening, always listening even in his sleep, for the moan of an animal
injured in the hunt, the cry of a female heavy with
unborn puppies. Morning meant rising ahead of the
sun to feed his wards with refuse from the castle
kitchen. The baron was prodigal with his food — at
his table, at least — and the waste was mountainous.
Stephen would break the bones into bitable size, dis-

card the tainted or tough, and try to please the palate of every dog: pork for Caius, mutton for Julius and Nero. . . . He shared the food with his dogs. Accustomed to cheese and bread, he now ate meat.

He was never invited to join a hunt; after all, he was Saxon, villein, and dog boy in descending order, and his duties strictly confined him to the castle. Whenever he saw the Baron affixed to his horse like the human half of a Centaur, he brought the swiftest hounds to accompany him — zealous to run and flush; patient to hold at bay for the Baron's spear.

The dogs without exception loved and obeyed him; Ralph and his knights generally ignored him. A sign, said John, that they approved of his work, since his predecessor had received a frequent cuffing before his unaccountable and permanent disappearance. One morning, after a particularly successful hunt — three deer, a fox, and a large boar — the Baron remarked to Stephen in the offhand way which was his closest approach to warmth:

"The dogs are running well."

It was Stephen's first and only compliment. He did not need, however, to be complimented on caring for friends, and he was quietly ecstatic when John, that best of friends, visited the kennels in his father's absence. Slender rather than skinny, the boy wore a green tunic which fell to his knees and kindled the lights in his greener-than-sparrowgrass eyes. His black hair curled above his ears and fell down his back like a cluster of grapes. Against all custom, including that of Stephen, he bathed at every chance from a laver and ewer. He walked in a pleasant redolence of ink, grass, and columbine.

Shyly he touched the kneeling Stephen's back. "Can I help?"

"No problems, John. Caius here has a thorn in his paw. There now. I've got it. A mean one, wasn't it, old fellow? Run along now, it won't hurt long."

"Can we talk?"

No one except his mother had listened with such a unanimity of attention — eyes alert and comprehending; poised for the cry of assent, the quiet encouragement, the smile of approval; and his ears actually seemed to perk like those of a dog or a fox. Not that John resembled an animal. If anything, he resembled a valiant boy martyr in *The Books of Saints*: thin, pale, ascetic, beautiful, and worshipful. It never occurred to Stephen that he, not Christ, was the object of John's adoration. He had his pride, he had his way with animals, he had his way with girls (except for Miriam). Otherwise, he was a lowly dog boy who would like to be a squire and then a knight. But John was a *saint*. It was up to Stephen to see that his friend did not become a martyr to a glowering father, lumpish varlets, or skulking Mandrakes.

Thanks to John and the dogs, he would not have regretted his life except that his parents — his last image of them branded into his memory as if by the King's chief torturer — were rarely out of his mind, never out of his nightmare-ridden sleep. The tall

square keep with its four turrets and its low fore-
building, its stories blackened by time and siege fires,
bristled above him like a huge Manticore. He longed
for the little cottage, the windowseat, the garland of
daffodils.

Grief, to be sure, was not continuous; tears were
rare; there were times of forgetting. There were even
consolations like the rising of a chill gray mist above
a moor to reveal the purple heath, a partridge nest,
the tracks of a fox. But he did not forget his purpose
to kill the murderers of his parents, and John, the
scholar, promised to turn warrior and follow him into
the fray.

"I wounded a wolf once," he recalled. "I hit it in
the snout with a stone and it changed its mind about
eating me. Those Mandrakes who — who — killed
your parents . . . they were worse than a wolf. At least,
I could throw some stones at them, if I had the
chance."

"And use a sling. I'll teach you how," said Stephen.
"But what we need is a guide."

"To lead us to their warrens?"

"Exactly."

"A virgin. Nothing else will do. Or so the Chaplain
says. But how will you know which three Mandrakes
to kill? You only saw their backs in the moonlight,
didn't you?"

"Doesn't matter. We'll kill anything that looks like
a tree and walks like a man! If we miss the three

murderers, well, at least we'll make the forest safer for travelers."

John, however, had reservations. "They live as they must," he said. "Except for the ones who killed your parents, why can't we leave them to their warrens?"

"Afraid, little friend? You can always stay in the castle."

"I'm going with you," said John, "but I think there ought to be a reason for killing something. We don't kill Saracens because of their dark skins, do we? It's because they dishonored Christ by stealing his home and his sacred relics."

"Forgive me, John. I know you aren't afraid." It was easy to recognize and respect compassion in his friend. It was hard to cultivate the quality in himself and distinguish between three particular murderers and a murderous race. After all, he had championed a little girl, whose people had promptly and savagely killed his mother and father.

"The biggest problem," he said, "is finding a virgin."

John confessed surprise. "The Church is very clear about fornication. I rather supposed that most of the girls in the village were virgins."

"Most aren't."

"Well, you must know the ones who are. Everybody seems to be your, er, friend."

"That's my problem," said Stephen. "I've too many female friends, and when you consider the other boys, and allow at least one girl for each boy — and that's conservative — well, how many virgins are left? I can count them on one hand." (It was the only way he could count.)

"Possibly a few of the girls pleasure most of the boys," suggested John, who looked upon virginity as something tangible, like a gem from the Holy Land, "a pearl of great price." Stephen had stolen many gems, but Stephen was his friend; therefore, he reasoned, the girls were to blame, like the careless cottager who forgets to bolt her door.

"Most of the girls pleasure all of the boys." Then, he added tactfully, "Boys over twelve, that is. Have I sung my Unicorn Song for you?"

"No. Is it a ballad?"

"You might call it that. Mother helped me with the rhymes."

His voice was loud if unmelodious:

To trap the grave-eyed unicorn,
Our monks and scribes assure,
A knight needs not a hunting horn
But a virgin for his lure.

The quarry with the doleful eyes
Has not been seen of late.
I wonder if the shortage lies
In unicorns — or bait.

"Now we must find the bait," said John. "There *is* Miriam," said Stephen. "Though I hate to put her in danger, I think she qualifies."

"If she's turned you down, she must have turned down everybody else."

Stephen reconsidered her qualifications. "But I'm not the only eel in the marsh. Big Thomas used to pursue her night and day, and she rather seemed to like him. She used to meet him at night under the Merlin Tree. I asked her about him once, and she said she was trying to save his soul. But you never know what method an inexperienced girl will use." Since the castle Chaplain preached incredibly dull sermons which condemned *all* earthly pleasures, he lost the chance to effectively condemn any pleasure; and what with the Baron's example, the power of the Church was slight in the village and castle. Furthermore, there were few recreations except for knucklebones and Hoodman Blind, which could hardly compare to "gathering rosebuds."

"We'll just have to ask her," said John.

"Just like that? Girls have their pride."

"You don't want to waste any time, do you? You've been a dog boy for nearly two months now."

With the help of the gatekeeper Antony, a young man who had inadvertently made their quest more difficult, Stephen arranged a meeting with Miriam under the Merlin Tree. It was Antony to whom he had given Bucephalus and who allowed him to leave the castle, from time to time, and visit his dog.

"I'm coming too," announced John.

Stephen shook his head. "She won't tell if both of us are there."

"I've studied dialectic. I can trick the truth out of her. You get tongue-tied sometimes at awkward moments." In spite of his shyness, John was far more eloquent than his father, the Baron, who generally spoke in grunts.

"I just don't know —"

"Which is more important, finding a virgin or saving a girl's pride?" John's shyness, it seemed, concealed an inflexible will.

"Very well then. Tonight."

Miriam emerged, smiling, from a copse of sycamore trees and froze in her tracks, as if she had met a wolf or an amphisbaena.

The son of her liege lord!

Stephen was quick to explain: "I've brought my friend. I wanted you to meet him."

Looking as elusive as a moonbeam, and as likely to dissolve with the first passing cloud, Miriam offered a tremulous hand.

"I am pleased to meet you, John."

John was poised and confident. "I hear you own a *History of the Kings of Britain.*"

"Yes, I do. I've read it, oh, it must be a dozen times." It was rare for a villein's family to own a codex. Miriam was justly proud.

"My father has *Plutarch's Lives.*"

The night was hushed of cicadas, silent of thrushes,

sweet with early summer. It was a night for confidences. Instead, *codices!* Dialectic, however effective, was certainly dull.

"Cleopatra is my favorite queen," she announced. Stephen's knowledge of ancient queens was miserly, if not miniscule. He knew, though, that Cleopatra had married a number of times, enjoyed innumerable lovers, and died from the bite of an asp on her breast. The region of the bite suggested a certain laxity in her morals.

"Wasn't she a bit free with her favors?" John pursued.

"Oh, great queens have privileges. I suppose you mean Caesar and Antony. Most women would have yielded to one or the other."

"But to both?" asked John. "It seems a bit, well, indiscriminate." (*Must* he use such unfamiliar words?) "And there *were* others."

"Between, not during," said Miriam with a touch of asperity.

"But when she thought Antony had forsaken her —"

"He had for awhile. He married Octavia in Rome. Can you blame Cleopatra for consoling herself with Egyptian gallants? And even then she was true to Antony in her soul."

Stephen stifled a yawn. The loves of a dead queen interested him considerably less than the loves of a live Miriam, and not those of her soul.

"And when Octavius made advances —"

41

"Miriam," Stephen blurted. "What do you think of the Mandrakes?"

"I'm afraid of them," she gasped. A leap of twelve hundred years was not conducive to organized conversation. "Isn't everyone? And you especially have cause —"

"That's what I'm getting at. I want to find the ones who killed my parents."

"You'll never find them in the forest. They live in warrens, you know. Or stand so still you mistake them for a tree. I don't see how —"

"But if we had a unicorn to guide us and fight with us —"

"You know how rare they are."

"Have you ever seen one?" interjected John, looking a trifle annoyed with Stephen for interrupting his devious but promising inquisition.

"No, never. But I don't go into the forest when I can help it. And when I do go, it's usually with my father and brothers to feed the swine, and the swine make a lot of racket, and —"

"Stephen, she's *never* seen a unicorn," said John.

"Miriam, will you lead us?"

"I'd be terribly afraid, I'd —"

"Are you or aren't you?" Stephen cried, distracted beyond endurance. Talking around the Maypole, that's what it was!

"Am I what, Stephen?"

"A virgin, what else? Did you think I meant a Mandrake?"

42

She gave him a wistful stare. "You ought to know the answer to that, Stephen," and, proud as Eleanor of Aquitaine marching into exile, she turned and strode away from them.

"She may not do," said John. "Any girl who admires Cleopatra that much —" his disappointment was obvious. He had definitely liked the girl.

"Miriam," Stephen called after her, with a mixture of shame and desperation. "It's for my parents' sake. That's why we had to question you."

She stopped, hesitated, and returned to them with slow, deliberate steps. She took Stephen's face between her hands and kissed him on the cheek. It was one of her sisterly kisses.

"My poor Stephen. Of course I'll help you find your unicorn. I promise you my qualifications are beyond question."

IV

"The forest?" he cried. "To hunt for Mandrakes? Do you want to risk your necks? Or should I say your blood?"

"Not *any* Mandrakes, Antony. *The* Mandrakes," explained John. "The ones who —"

"I know, I know,'" the gatekeeper sighed. He had the look of a spaniel with cropped ears and melancholy eyes: put-upon but reliable. "The Baron's gone to visit his friend in the Castle of the Boar. Won't

45

be back for a week. Go on your expedition then. But *you* be back in a day."

Antony pushed a lever which turned a wheel which opened the gates like the jaws of Leviathan.

"I feel," said Miriam, "as if we were going to be eaten. You know, I told my mother I was taking a posset to a friend. Do you think the posset is me?" Miriam's mother was stout, kindly, and not in the least suspicious. She could read a codex or recite an incantation, but she knew of Stephen only as "the rogue with the girls," and never guessed that the rogue was taking *her* girl into the forest.

"Balderdash," said Stephen. "Once we find our unicorn — and that's your job, Miriam — we'll be as safe as the Pope in the Vatican."

"What I'm afraid of," said John, "is a premature dinner." He turned to Antony. "Will you feed Stephen's dogs? Otherwise, the Baron will punish him."

Another sigh and a yes.

"And Bucephalus," added Stephen. "You never forget to feed *him,* do you?"

"No," said Antony. "He eats better than I do, and a great deal more. Now be on your way before I change my mind."

Like Pilgrims bound for Jerusalem — frightened, doubtful of reaching their goal, but matching ignorance with determination — they entered the deepest forest west of Germany. Stephen and John wore identical green tunics; Stephen carried a bow, John a sling which Stephen had taught him to use. Miriam carried a lantern in case they were forced to spend a night in the wilds. Arrayed in her usual ankle-long robe of brown homespun, she was also, said Stephen, "cloaked in virginity."

"It won't stop any arrows," she said.

"It's stopped a great many," he muttered under his breath.

By daylight the edge of the forest was eerie but not alarming. Woodsmen chopped the trees and farmers drove the swine in search of pannage or edible roots. But edge became interior; oak and elm and sycamore hoary with moss, like a great dark net, filtered the sun into fitful flickerings, allowing a meadow, a circlet of daisies, a stream, but thickening, darkening, lowering, as if to entangle the youthful adventurers.

"A road!" cried Miriam. "In the midst of the forest."

"The Stane," said Stephen with bland authority. It did not become a leader to show surprise.

"It leads from Chichester to London," said John. "The Romans built it and the Monks still patrol it."

"It's not for us," said Stephen. "Can you imagine a unicorn on a road? Here now, back into the woods with you. We must just stroll along casually, and let them sniff us out."

"I expect we should talk," said Miriam. "Otherwise, we'll seem to be hunting. John, who do you think was the greatest ruler among the ancients?"

"Julius Caesar."

(Stephen fretted to name Alexander.)

"And Cleopatra used him for all he was worth."

"He used *her.* Do you really think he meant to make her his queen? And when he was stabbed, she hadn't a chance with Octavius."

"Alexander," Stephen announced with finality.

"No, Stephen, it was Octavius who beat her. Later he was called Augustus."

"I know that, John." (He knew no such thing). "But if we're talking about ability, we have to mention Alexander, don't we? I simply wanted to say that he conquered more land and more women than anyone else, including Caesar. He must be the greatest."

"More land but not more women. *No* women, the Chaplain says."

Unexpectedly they plunged into a dark well of sheer, unbroken forest, rather like falling out of a boat and into the sea. Ancient rulers, even though one of them had built the Stane, seemed remote and unimportant. There was scarcely a hole in the net of leaves above them, scarcely a twinkle of sun.

"Hush," said Stephen. "We don't want to frighten the unicorn. This is the kind of place they like the best."

Fear was almost tangible in the air, like the inky cloud of a squid. Stephen had never seen the ocean or learned to swim. But this is a sea, he thought. The trees are sharks. The vines are octopi. We will surely perish without our unicorn, our dolphin of the woods.

John turned as pale as a mariner drowned in a storm, and Miriam clutched at his hand. There was no more talk of ancient kings and queens. Another royalty ruled or fought in this wood.

"Do you think," said Miriam, "we should spend the night in the forest? We haven't any coverlets. Even in summer, the nights can be cold. Besides, my mother will wonder where I am."

"We must look for a hollow tree," said Stephen. "It's much too late to start for home. Besides, what have we found? Not even a hoofprint. One of us can stand watch while the other two sleep."

"What will we eat?" asked John. He was not accustomed to sharing a meal with dogs.

"First we'll find a nest, then we'll think about dinner. See this bulge in my tunic? I've a pouch, with bread and cheese and a flagon of beer!"

"And here's our tree," said domestic Miriam. "Lightning has hollowed it out. See? Not one chamber but two, and carpeted with leaves. Almost as if a woodsman had come ahead of us to make our beds."

"And don't I hear a stream?" asked John. "It sounds like a basilisk shedding its skin. There. I see it through the trees."

"You can take your daily bath," smiled Stephen.

"Will you come with me?"

"I must see to the provisions." Water to Stephen was meant to drink.

"For once I think I'll skip my bath."

"You may catch the plague."

"The water looks cold," said John, eying the dark sinuosity of the stream. "Let's eat."

They kindled Miriam's lantern and made their

supper on bread and cheese. John, who had never drunk beer, began to talk so rapidly that Stephen accused him of sounding like the Chaplain, whereupon he declared the assassination of Caesar to be the most disastrous event in Roman history and began to recite from the *Gallic Wars:* "All Gaul is divided into three parts. . . ."

"Miriam, you stand the first watch," said Stephen. "It's the easiest. Then you can sleep the rest of the night."

She took up her stance like a Knight of the Temple and bravely extinguished the lantern.

"We're lucky," she said. "There's one little place where the moon comes through the trees."

"Of course," said Stephen. "You're my Moon Girl, aren't you?"

"For that you deserve a kiss."

He hopefully offered his mouth but Miriam sought his cheek.

Curiously, the kiss lingered in his dream, but hard and moist and prickly like a thorn. He opened his eyes and found that the kiss was not a dream. Someone had made a nest of his arms. Miriam? Had she tricked him about her qualifications?

He jumped to his feet and a little girl, definitely not Miriam, tumbled out of his arms and onto the leaves.

"An' you please, Sir, I am lost in the forest," she said.

In the watery light of the moon, he saw her rosebud

lips, her big, expectant eyes. His burning cheek revealed her race.

"What do you want?" he cried.

"Shelter and warmth, if I may."

"Which is your village?"

"It hasn't a name," she faltered. Her voice was sweet, her English quaint but correct. Perhaps she had failed to pass with human parents and been returned to the woods, her original home.

"Miriam!" he called. John, tired to the bone,, continued to sleep. Miriam, stooping to enter the tree, stared with chagrin at the little girl.

"Did she slip past me?"

"Yes."

"A Mandrake?"

"Yes."

"I must have dozed. What will we do with her?"

"Get rid of her," he said. He could hardly murder a child. He still had his strength; she had only begun to sup. He carried her out of the tree and aimed her toward the stream.

"Go home," he said.

"Would you chase me into the forest?" she wailed.

With a tap to her bottom, he said, "Find your parents. You know the forest better than I do." She looked him a sad reproach and skittered among the trees. He felt as if he had beaten one of his hounds.

"Stephen, I'm sorry. I make a terrible adventuress, don't I?"

"You were very tired," he said. "It couldn't be

helped. I'll take the rest of your watch."

"Do you think we've happened on one of their lairs? Some of them live in trees instead of warrens, you know."

"If we have, may Alexander send us a unicorn." He could not resist a hint of reproach.

"We'll find one tomorrow," she promised. "I won't fail you again. They're shy, remember. They've probably been looking us over and, uh, testing me."

"Go to sleep now, Stephen. I'll take over." John, thin but authoritative, materialized from the tree.

Stephen described the girl. "A winsome child but a Mandrake, take my word. I think we should both stand watch."

The moon, occasionally visible through the branches, climbed the sky like a giant lethargic snail.

"Sleep now, John. You'll need your strength in the morning."

"Will you be my pillow?"

"Cold, little friend?"

"A bit."

Stephen enfolded him with a protective arm. "Pretend I'm a brazier warm with coals."

"If you don't mind, I'll leave you as Stephen." He paused. "You see, I'm not really cold. I'm scared. I have been ever since we left the castle, only it got worse after dark. I'm afraid to sleep. Nightmares, don't you know."

"I do know, and I'm scared too," admitted Stephen. "But two fears, they say, can join to make a courage."

"If I'm one of the fears," said John, "I must be part of the courage. For awhile, though, I felt — uncompanioned."

"Never say that again — not with me."

"Stephen, did you know there were trees so close to us here? I thought we were in a tiny clearing. But look — there are trees — what do you think they are? Small sycamores, perhaps?"

Mandrakes!

There was not even time to lift a bow. It was hand to hand, but the Mandrakes had many hands. You could kick at their legs and they recoiled like a man. But their tendrils lashed your eyes and clogged your ears and made you think of a walking octopus. Stephen was much the strongest boy in the village; stronger, even, than most of the men. He had saved a lamb from a hungry wolf. He had saved a girl from a band of rapacious lepers. He had not been fearless by any means, but fear had given him strength.

It would take a Samson, however, to fight these moving trees. In a sense, they epitomized the inscrutable forest, its mystery, its mastery. When the Romans had built their road, they had battled wolves and savages blue with woad, but not the Mandrakes, not the forests within the forest.

He thought of John and Miriam — he had led them to their deaths.

He did not fall, he was flung to the ground by the lash of a tentacle. Weight on his chest; tendrils in his mouth; simply to breathe became his one concern.

"Alexander," he prayed in his mind. "You conquered Tyre, Persia, and Egypt too. You marched through an Indian Hell and almost reached the sea. Help your disciple to breathe. Help him to rise and help his friends!"

Miriam answered his prayer. Lunging out of the tree, she cried at the top of her lungs:

"Unicorn, save us!"

His head lay in Miriam's lap. She smelled of roots and thyme, and her hand, unspeakably soft, was bathing his brow with a cloth she had torn from her gown.

"John is fine. So am I. How do you feel?"

"Planted," he said. "Thrown in a hole with the dirt piled on top of me."

"Never mind," she smiled. "You won't sprout rootlets. The Mandrakes are gone — two of them, at least. The third is our captive."

It was day and the sun had found holes in the net of leaves, scattering the earth with ingots of gold.

"But the unicorn is here."

His horn was mother-of-pearl; his gossamer fur was streaked and torn, but he held a powerful hoof on the fallen foe. He looked at Stephen with warm, intelligent eyes.

"He must have been standing guard from the first," she said. "I thought I glimpsed him before we found our tree. You ought to have seen him rout the Mandrakes! Poor little John was blue from lack of breath. They *do* like to suffocate. And you — I almost gave you up when I saw you there on the ground. But then *he* came. And you see what he did."

"We'll call him Alexander," said Stephen.

"He'll like that," said Miriam, and then, domestic even in crisis, she started to build a fire.

Stephen climbed to his feet, decided that none of his aches meant a broken bone, and hunched beside the fire to regain his strength.

Porridge! It was only a wish.

He thought of another cook, a tidier kitchen than out-of-doors.

"Cheese is all we have," said Miriam. "We ate the bread last night, and John finished the beer."

"Look at his horn," said John. "It curves like a scimitar. And see how it catches the sun. Do you think he would fancy some cheese?"

"No," said Stephen, hungrily eying the remnants. "It's much too coarse for such an ethereal animal." (John had taught him the lofty adjective.)

"At least we can ask," said Miriam. "Unicorn, do you fancy a bite of cheese?"

"He can't understand," said Stephen.

Daintily but decisively, the unicorn nibbled the last, lingering morsels from Miriam's hand.

"Will you guide us on our quest?"

The animal bent his head to Miriam's touch.

"He's taken a special liking to you," said John.

"I expect it's my qualification. You know, it always seemed useless before. It made me wonder what I had missed."

"A lot," said Stephen, "but lucky for us. And now for the Mandrake. We shall have to kill him, of course."

"But we don't even know that he's one of the murderers," protested John.

"He tried to murder *us,* didn't he?"

"Yes, but I think we stole his lair and frightened his relative."

"Never mind, he's one of *them.*"

The Mandrake exuded a green liquid from his wounds. Fallen, he did not resemble a tree; he resembled a shaggy boy with green hair and white skin. A big boy, though; and soon to be grown. Already a killer; soon to be able to kill in spite of unicorns.

"He's not going anywhere just yet," said Miriam. "Alexander will guard him while we bathe in the stream. John is so clean he makes me feel like a scullery maid."

By daylight, it was one of those gently twisting streams which make you think of a path instead of a snake. Reeds grew along the banks; cattails too, straight as a shepherd's staff, but brown and soft at the top.

Modest Miriam bathed apart from the boys, the reeds a screen between them.

"I hope she can't hear me," said Stephen. "I never told her I don't know how to swim."

"It isn't deep. Here, give me your hand."

Christ, how sweet the water felt — cool, not cold, and deep but not deep enough to drown! He might

56

even learn to like a bath. He scraped a handful of fur from the cattail stalks. "It's good for wounds," he said, and he rubbed it carefully over his battered friend. His mother had taught him the remedy after his bout with the wolf.

"Now," he said, a catch in his throat. "I guess we must kill the Mandrake and be on our way."

"But what will the little girl do? He's probably her brother."

"That's not our worry."

"I rather think the ones who killed your parents were the family of the child who was killed at the fair."

"But I tried to help her."

"They wouldn't know that."

"Well, I am going to kill him just the same. He tried to kill *us*, didn't he?"

"When he found us in his lair."

The wounded Mandrake looked at him with eyes surprisingly human, and human contours curved beneath his foliage of green. Naked, filthy, murderous — but still a boy. Except for an accident of birth, he might have been Stephen's friend, owned a dog, lived in a villein's hut.

"God's Bowels," swore Stephen, kneeling and rubbing some cattail fur in the creature's wounds. The boy relaxed under Stephen's touch. His eyes grew soft; he tried to speak, but his words were unintelligible.

Stephen leaped to his feet and, without a backward

glance, strode from the tree and summoned his friends. "Come on now. It's time to go."

"Home?" asked Miriam.

"That might be best." (He was sure it was best.) "We've eaten or drunk our provisions and wasted our strength. We can come another time."

Stubborn as Balaam's ass, the unicorn blocked their path.

"He wants us to follow him," cried John.

"Must we?" asked Miriam. "We've seen him. Isn't that enough?"

"He's probably angry I didn't kill the Mandrake," said Stephen. "We'd better do what he wants."

"Stephen," said John, taking his hand. "You did what you must. It wasn't in you to kill him, helpless like that. I'm proud of you."

"I'm not proud of myself. You've made me woman-ish, that's what you've done, both of you. The least I can do is follow the unicorn."

V

He seemed to see an immensity of light — solid, unbroken, impenetrable. He stumbled out of the forest ahead of his friends and behind the unicorn and threw up his hands at the sudden, hurtful brilliance. He seemed to hear the roaring of many fires. It was the light which spoke, sang, whispered in secret tongues. The dark forest, the pastel glades, had led to another country. A country which seemed to float in a nimbus blending earth and sky, gradually breaking into individual facets, the meadow of yellow flowers, jonquil, daisy, daffodil — spring prolonged into summer; summer anticipating fall — the sunlight dripping from the black surrounding trees which enclosed the light like a wall.

In the midst of the burning grazed the unicorns: a herd of them, perhaps a dozen, stag, doe, newborn calf, safe in their island of sunlight, secure from encroachment of forest and Mandrake — soft of fur, large-eyed, kind-eyed, kingly-eyed, lifting their horns to greet the approach of their friend and those he had brought to them out of the forest.

Alexander hurried to join his comrades. He began a communion of eyes, telling, no doubt, of a hollow tree, friends, a battle beneath an ivory moon.

"It's the Valley of the Unicorns." John, hushed and reverent, spoke in a whisper. To shout might have scattered the herd to the winds from which they seemed to have drawn their grace.

"But of course," said Miriam, walking to meet the herd. "We searched and now we have found." She stroked the fur of their soft, uplifted muzzles.

"Stephen," said John. "They expect us, don't you see?" He tugged at Stephen's arm.

"You, not me," said Stephen. "They won't even meet my eyes." Of course. He had spared the Mandrake boy.

"Alexander!" cried John. "You've brought us to meet your friends!" He ran to join the herd. Greener than green-o-the-woods, he flickered among the russet animals, touching a muzzle, stroking a calf.

"Stephen, look! They aren't afraid at all."

Stephen, beloved of animals, dog boy to the Baron, idol to Bucephalus, moved invisibly into the herd. He opened his mouth to speak and they moved away from him. He raised a hand to caress and touch the air.

They are angry with me, he thought. I did not kill their foe.

No, not angry . . . indifferent.

I failed. An avenging angel, I sheathed my sword. My mercy was nothing but cowardice. I would have spared Sodom, Gomorrah, the world before the Flood.

Heaven and Earth, immortal spirit and mortal flesh — some men combine these and rise above the rest. They become strong and great enough to follow a star, a voice, a Grail to the Holy Land. Did Richard remain in England to count his gold? He fought for Jerusalem! My spirit is shackled by flesh. Mandrakes are born of the Earth, indifferent to Heaven; they climb from the dirt, they walk in slime and they cannot see the stars. And I am one of them. . . .

He felt the weariness of those forgotten by God; the walk through the forest, the long watch, the little sleep, the fight by the hollow tree. Here was sustenance, but not for him. Here was wonderment, but only for his friends. He spun to the edge of the clearing, fell to his knees, and watched his happy friends. A youthful Christ, John had lifted a lamb in his slender arms. Miriam, Moon Girl and saint, sat on the daisied grass, and the animals bowed to receive her caresses, laying their heads in her lap.

"Is it fair?" he wanted to shout. John had asked him to spare the Mandrake's life. Ah, but John was a softhearted little boy; he, Stephen, must share a man's burden, accept a man's guilt.

("Vengeance is mine," said the Lord.)

He buried his face in the grass and, through his tears, he watched a grasshopper moving his slow, deliberate way across the field.

"Grasshopper, be my friend!"

The grasshopper leaped to a neighboring blade of grass, which bent beneath his weight; leaped to the sturdy tower of a daffodil, and Stephen, earthbound, felt the fire of his wounds, the painful pressing of grass against bruised flesh. My wounds will heal, he thought, but the fire of shame is unquenchable even into eternity.

A shadow fell across him like a shroud. John, he thought. Miriam. Come to lead me into the herd. I do not want them to see my tears.

"Go away," he cried. He smelled a fragrance of herbs and felt a warmth which was not from the sun.

Blinking, he raised his head to confront a unicorn. She smelled of bergamot. Grace was her curving flank, her horn upheld with pride but not presumption. Age had enriched her instead of withering her flanks.

She lowered her head and pressed his burning cheek. He held her against his breast and felt the beat, beat, beat of her answering heart.

He must make her a gift. But what had a villein's son, Saxon and dog boy, to offer a unicorn?

"Here," he cried, breaking a daffodil from its stalwart stalk, "and here, and here." He strung them into a wreath with a piece of vine and placed them on her head.

"It isn't much," he said. "I would give you the Holy Grail if I knew where to find it."

She looked at him with grave, loving, and familiar eyes. . . .

"Shall we tell anyone what we saw?" asked John as they neared the village and the workaday-world, the power of the Baron, the sermons of his priest.

"No one would believe us."

"Did we really see what we think?" asked Miriam. "It seemed so — wondrous."

"We saw it," said Stephen.

"Shall we ever go back?"

"We don't need to. It's enough to know that"— he started to say "she"—"that they're there."

"We didn't kill any Mandrakes," said Miriam.

"The best journeys are those whose ends can't be foreseen."

"Stephen, you sound like a poet," said John. "You even look different."

"What do you mean, John?"

"It's as if you've brought some of the brightness back with you."

"It's only the sun," he said.

"No. It's as if you wore a garland of daffodils."

Part Two: John

I

The Plague, I have heard, is a white old man with halting steps and trembling hands. In the marketplace, he limps on a cane like a leper and begs for a tarnished penny, a scrap of cheese.

"Go away!" you shout. "I have no alms for death!"

But when he chooses to strike—! Why, then his cane is as swift and cruel as a sword.

It was not a leper who visited Miriam. She described him to Stephen and John:

"He came in the night. I think he is Hermes, guide to the souls of the dead. There was such a brightness about him! He made me remember our unicorns."

Impetuous Stephen seized her hand. Gently she drew away from him. "He has come for *me*. For you and John, there are other journeys, I think, another guide. Perhaps Jerusalem. . . ."

And they found their guide, but no one knew if she came from Heaven or Hell. God, I felt, had made me his instrument. It was I who must judge. Did I judge her ill?

It was I who sheltered them from the Mandrake Folk. Loved them, hurt them, and then at the last . . . but you shall judge me as I judged her.

He ran blinded by tears across the heath, startling birds into flight, pheasants and grouse enough to feast a king. Conies peered from their nests and submerged like frogs in a pond with a dull, simultaneous plop. Didn't they know that he, timorous John, who had lost his bow in the woods and scattered the arrows out of his quiver, was not a creature to fear? He had come from the hunt with his father, lord of the black-keeped castle called The Tortoise, and the knights Robert, Arthur, Edgar, and the rest. The names of the knights were different, their features almost identical. Rough hands, calloused from wielding swords against the Infidel — and their fellow Englishmen. Cheeks ruddy with mead and not with the English climate. Odorous bodies enveloped by furlined surcoats which they pridefully wore even in the flush of summer, instead of imitating the villeins with their simple breechclouts or their trousers without tunics. Lank, sweat-dampened hair, long in the back and cut in a fringe across their foreheads.

John, the Baron's son, had been allowed the first shot at a stag beleaguered by hounds. He was not a good bowman, but the stag had been much too close to miss except by design. He had missed by design. Once, gathering chestnuts with his friend Stephen, the shepherd, he had seen the same animal, a splendid beast with horns like wind-beaten trees along the North Sea.

"He isn't afraid of us," Stephen had whispered.

"Nor has he reason to be," said John. "We would never harm him. He's much too beautiful."

Now, the animal had turned and looked at him with recognition, it seemed, and resignation; harried by hounds; bemused in a clump of bracken. John had fired his arrow above the antlers. The stag had escaped, bursting out of the bracken as if the coarse ferns were blades of grass and leveling three dogs with his adamantine hooves.

"Girl!" his father had shouted, hoarse with rage at losing a feast and a pair of antlers to grace his barren hall. "I should get you a distaff instead of a bow!"

For punishment John was bladed. After the knights had downed a smaller animal, a young doe, they had stretched him across the warm, bloody carcass and each man had struck him with the flat of his sword. Most of the knights had softened their blows. After all, he was their liege lord's son. But his father's blow had left him bleeding and biting his tongue to hold back shameful tears.

Then they had left him.

"Go to the kennels and get your friend Stephen to dry your tears," his father had sneered. A coarse guffaw greeted the taunt. Stephen was said to have lain with every villein's daughter between twelve and twenty, and men without daughters liked to jest: "Girls weep till Stephen dries their tears."

Alone in the woods, John forgot his shame; he was too frightened. Only twelve, he knew of desperate thieves, sentenced to die by the rope, who had taken refuge among the sycamores which remembered the Romans, and the oaks which had drunk the blood of Druid sacrifices. As for animals, there were wolves and bears and long-tusked boars, and amphisbaenas too, the twin-headed serpents, and griffins with scaly wings. Worst of all, there were the Mandrake People who, grown like roots, clambered out of the ground to join their kin in acts of cannibalism.

Where could he go? Not to the castle, certainly, where the hunters had doubtless climbed in a broad wooden tub to scrape the grime of weeks from each other's backs, while kitchen wenches doused them with buckets of steaming water and ogled their naked brawn. Once, the castle had held his mother. Its darkness had shone with the whiteness of her samite; its odors were masked with the cloves and the cinnamon, the mace and the musk of her kitchen; its bailey had bloomed with a damson tree whose seeds had come from the Holy Land, and delicate shallots, the "Onions of Ascalon," had reared their tender shoots around the tree, like little guardian gnomes.

"If there must be fruits of war," she had said, "we must see that they are living things, not dead, sweet things, not bitter, soft things, not hard. The verdure of earth and not the gold from dead men's coffers."

Six years ago she had died of the pox. Now, when he knelt on the stone floor of the chapel, he prayed to Father, Son, and Mary, but Mary was Mother.

No, he could not go to the castle. He could but he did not wish to visit the Abbot's cottage and face another lesson in logic and astrology, Lucan and Aristotle. He was a willing, indeed a brilliant scholar. But there were times to study and times to look for Stephen. In spite of his father's taunt, it was time to look for Stephen. It was not that his friend was soft or womanish like a sister. He was, in fact, as rough-swearing, ready-to-fight a boy as ever tumbled a girl in the hay. But he curbed his roughness with John, respected his learning, and ignored his weaknesses.

How could you best describe him? Angry, sometimes, but angry *for* things and not against them. For the serfs and the squalor in which they lived; the dogs which were run too hard in the hunt and gored by wild boars; the animals killed for sport and not for food. Sometimes, too, he was glad: loudly, radiantly, exuberantly keen on things — drawing a bow, feeding his dogs, swinging a scythe.

At other times he was neither angry nor glad, but beyond anger and gladness; enraptured by dreams: of meeting an angel or finding Excalibur or, best of all, buying his freedom and becoming a Knight Hospitaler to succor pilgrims and slaughter Infidels ("But you would have to take an oath of chastity," John reminded him. "I'll think about that when the time comes," said Stephen). Furthermore, he was one of those rarest of rarities, a dreamer who acts on his dreams, and lately he had talked about the ill-fated Children's Crusade, and how it was time for other Stephens, other Nicholases, to follow the first children and, armed with swords instead of crosses, succeed where they had failed.

"With Miriam dead," said Stephen, brushing a tear, "what is there to hold us here at The Tortoise? I have no family, and you have only a father who would rather blade you than talk to you."

It was John's unspeakable fear that Stephen would leave for Jerusalem without him, and yet he did not know if he had the courage for such a journey, through the dark Weald to London and then by ship to Marseilles and the ports of Outre-Mer, the Outer Land, the Saracen Land. Now, he quickened his pace and thought of arguments with which to dissuade his friend. He met old Edward scything in the Common Meadow; a tattered breechclout around his loins, his face and shoulders as coarse and brown as a saddle ridden from London to Edinburgh. Edward did not look up from his task, nor miss a stroke of the scythe. "Why look at the sky?" he liked to mutter. "It belongs to angels, not to serfs."

"Have you seen Stephen?" John asked.

Swish, swish, swish went the scythe, and the weeds collapsed as if they had caught the plague.

"HAVE YOU SEEN STEPHEN?"

"I'm not deaf," the old man growled. "Your father's taken my youth, my pigs, and my corn, but not my ears. Not yet, anyway. Your friend'll be losing his, though, 'less he does his work. He oughta be here in the Meadow right now."

"But where *is* he?" cried John in desperation.

"Making for the Roman Place with that look in his eyes. That's where he hides, you know. Daydreams. Didn't even speak to me."

The Roman Place. The ruin where the Romans had worshipped their sun-god, Mithras, in an underground vault. Later, by way of apology to the Christian God, the Saxons had built a timber church to conceal the spot and turned the vault into a crypt for their dead. During the Norman Conquest, women and children had hidden in the church, and the Normans had set a torch to the roof and burned the building with all of its occupants. The charred and misshapen remnants were almost concealed — healed, as it were — by flowering gorse, and a few blackened timbers, which thrust like seeking hands from the yellow flowers, summoned no worshippers to the buried gods.

A stranger would not suspect a vault beneath the gorse, but John parted the spiny branches and climbed through a narrow hole to a flight of stairs. A sacredness clung to the place, a sense of time, like that of a Druid stone which lichen had aged to a muted, mottled orange and which thrust at the stars as if to commune with them in cosmic loneliness. Here, the worshippers of Mithras had bathed themselves in the blood of the sacrificial bull and climbed through the seven stages of initiation to commune with the sun instead of the stars. A nasty pagan rite, said the Abbot, and John had asked him why Jehovah had ordered Abraham to sacrifice Isaac. "It was only a test," snapped the Abbot.

"But what about Jephthah's daughter? *She* wasn't a test." The Abbot had changed the subject.

Already, at twelve, John had begun to ask questions about the Bible, God, Christ, and the Holy Ghost. To Stephen, religion was feeling and not thought. God was a patriarch with a flowing beard, and angels were almost as real as the dogs in his kennel. With John it was different. Only the Virgin Mary was not a subject for doubts or arguments, but a beautiful, ageless woman robed in samite, dwelling in the high places of the air or almost at hand, outshining the sun and yet as simple as bread, grass, birds, and Stephen's love: invisible but never unreachable.

At the foot of the stairs he faced a long, narrow cave with earthen walls which contained the loculi of Christians buried in their cerements and which converged to the semi-circle of an apse. Now, the apse was empty of Mithras slaying the sacred bull and Mary holding the infant Christ. Stephen knelt in their place. He held a waxen candle which lit the frescoed roof: Jesus walking on water; multiplying loaves and fish; bidding the blind to see and the lame to walk.

"John," he gasped, "I have found —"

"A Madonna!"

She lay in a nest of bindweed shaped to a simple pallet. Her face was an ivory mask in the light of the candle. A carved Madonna, thought John, from the transept of a French cathedral, but flushed with the unmistakable ardors of life. No, he saw with a disappointment which approached dismay, she was much too young for the Virgin; a mere girl.

"An angel," said Stephen.

"An angel," sighed John, resenting her youthfulness. What did he need with a second angel, a girl at that? God (or the Virgin Mary) had sent him Stephen, angelic but not female and certainly not effeminate, his hair a riot instead of an aureole, his face more ruddy than pink: a Michael or Gabriel fit for sounding a trumpet instead of strumming a lyre.

The angel stirred and opened her eyes with a pretty fluttering; not with surprise or fright, but almost, thought John, with artful calculation, like some of the rustic lasses who flocked to Stephen's loft. Her teeth were as white as her linen robe, which was bound at the waist by a cord of cerulean silk. Her pointed slippers, unicorn leather trimmed with blue velvet, were such as might be worn in the soft pastures of heaven. She lacked only wings. Or had she concealed them under her robe? John was tempted to ask.

Stephen forestalled him. "Greet her," he whispered. "Welcome her!"

"In what language?" asked John sensibly. "I don't know the tongues of angels."

"Latin, I should think. She must know that, with all the priests muttering their Benedicites."

Stephen had a point. Rude English was out of the question, and also the French of the Normans, who, after all, had descended from barbarous Vikings.

"Quo Vadis?" asked John none too politely.

Her smile, though delectable, no doubt, to Stephen, did not answer the question.

"What are you doing here?" he repeated in Norman French.

Stephen, who understood some French, frantically nudged him. "You shouldn't question an angel. Welcome her! Worship her! Quote her a psalm or a proverb."

"We aren't sure she's an angel. She hasn't told us, has she?"

At last she spoke. "I do not know how I came here," she said in flawless Latin and, seeing the blankness on Stephen's face, repeated the words in English, but with a grave dignity which softened the rough tongue. At the same time, John noticed the crucifix which she held or rather clutched in her hands: a small Greek cross with arms of equal length, wrought of gold and encrusted with stones which he knew from his studies, though not from his father's castle, were the fabulous pearls of the East. "I remember only a darkness, and a falling, and a great forest. I wandered until I found the passage to this cave, and took shelter against the night. I must have been very tired. I feel as if I have slept for a long time." She lifted the cross and then, as if its weight had exhausted her slender hands, allowed it to sink becomingly against her breast.

"I suppose," said John with annoyance, "you're hungry."

Stephen sprang to his feet. "But angels don't eat! Can't you see, John? God has sent her to us as a sign! To lead us to the Holy Land! He took away Miriam, but sent us an angel to take her place. Stephen of France had his message from Christ. We have our angel."

"But look what happened to Stephen of France. Sold as a slave or drowned in the sea. Only the sharks know which."

"I don't think he's dead. And if he is, then he listened to the Devil's voice and not to God's. But we can *see* our angel."

"Indeed, you can see me," she said, "and you ought to see that I am famished. Angels do eat, I assure you — at least when they travel — and something more substantial than nectar and dew. Have you venison perhaps? Mead?"

"You must take her to the castle," said Stephen, clearly reluctant to part with his new-found angel.

"I've nothing so fine in the kennels."

"No," said John. "I'm not taking anyone to the castle. I've decided to stay with you in the kennels."

"Because of your father?"

"Yes. He bladed me before all of his men, and then he called me a —" He could not bring himself to repeat the taunt, especially to Stephen. "He called me a churl. Because I missed a stag. *Our* stag. The one we promised never to harm."

Stephen nodded with understanding. "I'm glad you missed him. They say he's the oldest stag in the forest. They say"— and here he lowered his voice — "that he isn't a stag at all, but Merlin turned to a beast by Vivian. But, John, how can you live with me in the kennels? It would wound your father's pride. A baron's son sharing a loft with a dog boy! He'd give you more than a blading, and as for me! You mayn't remember he cut off my father's ears because he broke a scythe. And now with an angel on our hands, the only thing to do is —"

"Get the angel off our hands?"

"Leave at once for the Holy Land. I have a little food in the kennels, a change of wear. You needn't go back to the castle at all. We've only to follow the Roman road through the Weald to London, and take ship to Marseilles, and from thence proceed to Outre-Mer."

"But Marseilles was where the French Stephen fell in the hands of slavers."

"But we have a guide! Miriam guided us to the unicorns, didn't she?"

"I liked Miriam better," muttered John. "If this one isn't really an angel —"

"At least we'll have made our escape from the castle."

"You mean we should leave the castle *forever*?" The prospect of leaving his father exhilarated him; he would feel like a falcon with its hood removed. But the castle held all of his possessions, his codex, *The Kings of Britain,* written on the finest vellum and bound between ivory covers; and the parchment containing his favorite poem, "The Owl and the Nightingale," copied laboriously by his own precise hand. Much more important, it held his mother's ghost, his sum of remembering: stairs she had climbed, tapestries woven, garments mended; his mother living in song what she could not live in life and singing of noble warriors and deathless loves:

*See, he who carved this wood commands me to ask
You to remember, oh treasure-adorned one,
The pledge of old . . .*

"Leave my father's castle," he repeated, "and not come back? Ever?"

Stephen's face turned as red as the Oriflamme, the fiery banner of the French kings. *"Your father's castle? This land belonged to my ancestors when yours were scurvy Vikings! You think I'll stay here forever as* dog boy and shepherd? Serving a man who blades his own son? Giving him what I grow and what I hunt, and asking his leave to take a wife? John, John, there's nothing for either of us here. Ahead of us lies Jerusalem!"

To Stephen, the name was a trumpet blast; to John a death knell. "But a forest stands in the way, and then a channel, and a rough sea swarming with Infidels. They have ships too, you know, swifter than ours and armed with Greek fire."

But Stephen had gripped his shoulders and fixed him with his blue, relentless gaze. "You know I can't leave you."

"You know you won't have to," sighed John.

The angel interrupted them, looking a little peeved that in their exchange of pleas and protestations, of male endearments, they were neglecting their quest and their inspiration. "As for leading you to the Holy Land, I don't even know this forest through which you say we must pass. But here in the ground it is damp, and before I came here, I did not like the look of the castle. It seemed to me dark and fierce, with a dry ditch and a gloomy keep, and narrow windows without a pane of glass. A fortress and not a home. If indeed I am an angel, I hope to find dwellings more pleasant here on earth. Or else I shall quickly return to the sky. In the meantime, let us set off for London, and you shall lead *me* until I begin to remember."

The angel between them, they climbed the stairs to the sun and, skirting old Edward, who was still busily scything in the Common Meadow, came at last to the kennels. It was mid-day. The Baron and his knights had remained in the castle since the hunt. His villeins, trudging out of the fields, had gathered in the shade of the water-mill to enjoy their gruel and bread. Had anyone noticed the quick, furtive passage of the would-be Crusaders, he would have thought them engaged in childish sports, or supposed that Stephen had found a young wench to share with his master's son and probably muttered, "It's high time."

While Stephen's greyhounds lapped at their heels, they climbed to his loft above the kennels to get his few belongings: two clover-green tunics with hoods for wintry days; wooden clogs and a pair of blue stockings which reached to the calf of the leg; a leather pouch bulging with wheaten bread and rounds of cheese; a flask of beer; and a knotted shepherd's crook.

"For wolves," said Stephen, pointing to the crook. "I've used it often."

"And Mandrakes," added John wickedly, hoping to frighten the angel.

"But we have no change of clothes for a girl," said Stephen.

"Never mind," she smiled, guzzling Stephen's beer and munching bread till she threatened to exhaust the supply before they began their journey. "When my robe grows soiled, I shall wash it in a stream and," she added archly, "the two of you may see if I am truly an angel."

The remark struck John as unangelic if not indelicate. As if they would spy on her while she bathed!

He longed for Miriam and her modesty; he never ceased to long for Miriam. (But she had died even as she lived, quietly, without fear or protest.) Not even the Plague could distort her sculptured face. "I will see you in Heaven," she said.

But Stephen reassured his angel. "We never doubted you were. And now——" A catch entered his voice. Quickly he turned his head and seemed to be setting the loft in order.

"We must leave him alone with his hounds," whispered John to the angel, leading her down the ladder.

A silent Stephen rejoined them in the Heath. His tunic was damp from friendly tongues and his face was wet, but whether from tongues or tears it was hard to say.

"You don't suppose," he said, "we could take one or two of them with us? The little greyhound without any tail?"

"No," said John. "My father will stomp and shout when he finds us gone, but then he'll shrug: 'Worthless boys, both of them, and no loss to the castle.' But steal one of his hounds, and he'll have his knights on our trail."

"Bucephalus?"

"You gave him to Antony. It wouldn't be fair to take him back. Not after all his help."

"But our angel has no name," cried Stephen suddenly and angrily, as if to say: "As long as she's come to take me from my hounds, she might at least have brought a name."

"I *had* a name, I'm sure. It seems to have slipped my mind. What would you like to call me?"

"Why not Ruth?" said Stephen. "She was always going on journeys in the Bible, leading cousins and such, wasn't she?"

"A mother-in-law," corrected John, who felt that, what with a Crusade ahead of them, Stephen should know the Scriptures.

"Leading and *being* led," observed the angel, whose memory, it seemed, had begun to return. "By two strapping husbands. Though," she hurried to explain, "not at the same time. Yes, I think you should call me Ruth."

She is much too young for Ruth, thought John, who guessed her to be about fifteen (though of course as an angel she might be fifteen thousand). The same age as Stephen, whose thoughts were attuned to angelic visions but whose bodily urges were not in the least celestial. Unlike a Knight Templar, he had made no vow of chastity. The situation was not propitious for a crusade in the name of God.

But once they had entered the Weald, the largest forest in southern England, he thought of Mandrakes and griffins instead of Ruth. It was true that the Stane, an old Roman highway, crossed the Weald to join London and Chichester — they would meet it within the hour — but even the Stane was not immune to the forest.

II

At Ruth's suggestion, they carefully skirted the grounds of a neighboring castle, the Boar's Lair.

"Someone might recognize John," she said. "Send word to his father."

"Yes," John agreed, staring at the Norman tower, one of the black wooden keeps built by William the Conqueror to enforce his conquest. "My father and Philip the Boar were once friends. Philip used to dine with us on Michaelmas and other feast days, and I played the kettledrums for him. Since then, he and my father have fallen out about their boundaries. They both claim a certain grove of beechnut trees—pannage for their swine. Philip wouldn't be hospitable, I'm sure."

Deviously, circuitously, by way of a placid stream and an old water wheel whose power no longer turned mill-stones and ground wheat into flour, they reached the Roman Stane. Once a proud thoroughfare for unconquerable legions, it had since resounded to Saxon, Viking, and Norman, who had used it for commerce and war but, unlike the conscientious Romans, never repaired the ravages of wheels and weather. Now, it had shrunk in places to the width of a peasant's cart, but the smooth Roman blocks, set in concrete, still provided a path for riders and walkers and great ladies in litters between two horses.

"I feel like the Stane," sighed Ruth, "much-trodden and a trifle weedy." She had torn the edge of her robe on prickly sedges and muddied the white linen. She had lost the circlet which haloed her head, and her silken tresses, gold as the throats of convolvulus flowers, had spilled like their trailing leafage over her shoulders. As for John, he was hot, breathless, and moist with sweat, and wishing that like a serf he dared to remove his long-sleeved tunic and revel in his breechclout.

"Stephen," Ruth sighed, "now that we've found the road, can't we rest a little?" Her speech, though still melodious, had relaxed into easy, informal English.

"We've just begun!" he laughed. "London lies days away. We want to be leagues down the road before night."

"But it's already mid-afternoon. Why not rest till it gets a little cooler?"

"Very well," he smiled, reaching out to touch her in good-humored acquiescence. Stephen, who found difficulty with words, spoke with his hands, which were nests to warm a bird, balms to heal a dog, bows to extract the music from swinging a scythe, wielding an ax, gathering branches to build a fire. He could gesture or point or touch with the exquisite eloquence of a man who was deaf, dumb, and blind. When you said good morning to him, he clapped you on the shoulder. When you walked with him, he brushed against you or caught you by the arm. He liked to climb trees for the rough feel of the bark or swim in a winter stream and slap the icy currents until he warmed his body. But he saved his touch for the things or the people he loved. Neither ugly things nor unkind people.

"We'll rest as long as you like," he said.

Ruth smiled. "I think I should borrow one of your tunics. You see how my robe keeps dragging the ground."

With a flutter of modesty she withdrew to a clump of bracken and changed to a tunic.

"Watch out for basilisks," John called after her. "Their bite is fatal, you know." He muttered under his breath to Stephen: "First she ate your food, and now she wears your clothes."

"Our food and clothes," reproved Stephen. "Remember we're Crusaders together."

John was shamed into silence. He had to listen to Ruth as she bent branches, snapped twigs, and rustled cloth, almost as if she wished to advertise the various stages of her change. He thought of the wenches—ten? twenty?—who had disrobed for Stephen. The subject of sexual love confused him. The Aristotelian processes of his brain refused to sift, clarify, and evaluate the problem; in fact, they crumpled like windmills caught in a forest fire. He had loved his mother—what was the word?—filially; Stephen he loved fraternally. But as for the other thing, well, he had not been able to reconcile the courtly code as sung by the troubadours—roses and guerdons and troths of deathless fidelity—and the sight of Stephen, surprised last month in his loft with a naked wench and not in the least embarrassed. Stephen had grinned and said: "In a year or so, John, we can wench together!" The girl, snickering and making no effort to hide her nakedness, had seemed to him one of those Biblical harlots who ought to be shorn or stoned. Who could blame poor Stephen for yielding to such allurements! As for himself, however, he had sworn the chivalric oath to practice poverty, chastity, and obedience to God. He had often thought of a monastery but rather than part with Stephen, who was not in the least monastic, he was willing to try a life of action.

"Has a crow got your tongue?" smiled Stephen. "I didn't mean to scold." He encircled John's shoulder with his arm. "You smell like cloves."

John stiffened, not at the touch but at what appeared to be an insinuation. He had not forgotten his father's taunt: "Girl!" According to custom, it was girls and women who packed their gowns in clove-scented chests, while the men of the castle hung their robes in the room called the *garderobe,* the lavatory cut in the wall beside the stairs, with a round shaft dropping to the moat. The stench of the shaft protected the room —and the robes—from moths.

"They belonged to my mother," he stammered. "The cloves, I mean. I still use her chest."

"My mother put flowering mint with her clothes," said Stephen. "All three gowns! I like the cloves better, though. Maybe the scent will rub off on me. I haven't bathed for a week." He gave John's shoulder a squeeze, and John knew that his manhood had not been belittled. But then, Stephen had never belittled him, had he? Teased him, yes; hurt him in play; once knocked him down for stepping on the tail of a dog; but never made light of his manliness.

"It's not a dangerous road," Stephen continued, talkative for once, perhaps because John was silent. "The abbots of Chichester patrol it for brigands. They don't carry swords, but Gabriel help the thief who falls afoul of their staves!"

"But the forest," John said. "It's all around us like a pride of griffins. With green, scaly wings. They look as if they're going to eat up the road. They've already nibbled away the edges, and"—he lowered his voice—

"she came out of the forest, didn't she?"

Stephen laughed. "She came out of the sky, simpleton! Didn't you hear her say she don't know nothing about the forest?"

Before John could lecture Stephen on his lapse in grammar, Ruth exploded between them, as green as a down in the tenderness of spring. She blazed in Stephen's tunic, its hood drawn over her head. She had bound her waist with the gold sash from her robe and discarding her velvet slippers, donned his wooden clogs, whose very ugliness emphasized the delicacy of her bare feet. She had bundled her linen robe around her slippers and crucifix.

"No one would ever guess that I'm an angel," she smiled. "Or even a girl."

"Not an angel," said Stephen appreciatively. "But a girl, yes. You'd have to roughen your hands and hide your curls to pass for a boy."

She made a pretence of hiding her hair, but furtively shook additional curls from her hood the moment they resumed their journey, and began to sing a familiar song of the day:

In a valley of this restless mind,
I sought in mountain and in mead . . .

Though she sang about a man searching for Christ, the words rippled from her tongue as merrily as if she were singing a carol. John wished for his kettledrums and Stephen began to whistle. Thus, they forgot the desolation of the road, largely untraveled at such an hour and looking as if the griffinscaly forest would soon complete its meal.

Then, swinging around a bend and almost trampling them, cantered a knight with a red cross painted on his shield — a Knight Templar, it seemed — and after him, on a large piebald palfrey, a lady riding pillion behind a servant who never raised his eyes from the road. The knight frowned at them; in spite of the vows demanded of his order, he looked more dedicated to war than to God. But the lady smiled and asked their destination.

"I live in a castle up the road," said John quickly in Norman French. Unlike his friends, he was dressed in the mode of a young gentleman, with a tunic of plum-colored linen instead of cheap muslin, and a samite belt brocaded with silver threads. Thus, he must be their spokesman. "I have come with my friends to search for chestnuts in the woods, and now we are going home."

The knight darkened his frown to a baleful glare and reined his steed, as if he suspected John of stealing a fine tunic to masquerade as the son of a gentleman. Boys of noble birth, even of twelve, did not as a rule go nutting with villeins whom they called their friends, and not at such an hour.

"We have passed no castle for many miles," he growled, laying a thick-veined hand on the hilt of his sword.

"My father's is well off the road, and the keep is

low," answered John without hesitation. "In fact, it is called The Tortoise, and it is *very* hard to break, like a tortoise shell. Many a baron has tried!"

"Mind you get back to The Tortoise before dark," the lady admonished. "You haven't a shell yourself, and the Stane is dangerous after nightfall. My protector and I are bound for the castle of our friend, Philip the Boar. Is it far, do you know?"

"About two leagues," said John, and he gave her explicit directions in French so assured and polished that no one, not even the glowering knight, could doubt his Norman blood and his noble birth. It was always true of him that he was only frightened in anticipation. Now, with a wave and a courtly bow, he bade them God-speed to the castle of the Boar, received a smile from the lady, and led his friends *away* from The Tortoise.

"Such a handsome lad," he heard the lady exclaim, "and manly as well."

"If I hadn't been so scared," said Stephen, once a comfortable distance separated them from the knight, his lady, and the unresponsive servant, "I'd have split my tunic when you said we were headed for The Tortoise. There isn't a castle for the next ten miles! It's the first fib I ever heard you tell."

"You were scared too?" asked John, surprised at such an admission.

"You can bet your belt I was! They were lovers, you know. Bound for a tryst at the castle of the Boar. He winks at such things, I hear. Runs a regular brothel for the gentry, including himself. That lady has a husband somewhere, and the Knight Templar might just have run us through to keep us from carrying tales."

With the fall of darkness, they selected a broad and voluminous oak tree, rather like a thicket set on the mast of a ship, and between them the boys helped Ruth to climb the trunk. With nimble hands she prepared a nest of leaves and moss in the crook of the tree and, having removed her clogs and hidden them, along with her crucifix, settled herself with the comfort of perfect familiarity. She seemed to have a talent for nests, above or below the ground. After she had eaten some bread and cheese and drunk some beer, she returned to the ground, stubbornly refusing assistance from either boy, and showed herself a more than adept climber.

"Is she angry with us?" asked John.

"She drank all that beer," explained Stephen, "and while she's gone —"

They scrambled to the edge of the nest and, bracing themselves against a limb, aimed at the next oak. Gleefully, John pretended that Ruth was crouching under the branches.

He was sorry to see her emerge from an elm instead of the inundated oak and rejoin them in the nest.

"I was looking for rushes to keep us warm," she said. "But I didn't find a single one. We'll have to lie close together." She chose the middle of the nest, anticipating, no doubt, a boy to warm her on either side, and Stephen obligingly stretched on her left.

With the speed and deftness of Lucifer disguised as a serpent, John wriggled between them, forcing Ruth to the far side of the nest. Much to his disappointment, she accepted the arrangement without protest and leaned against him with a fragrance of galangal, the aromatic plant imported from Outre-Mer and used as a base for perfume by the ladies of England.

"The stars are bright tonight," she said. "See, John, there's Arcturus peeping through the leaves, and there's Sirius, the North Star. The Vikings called it the Lamp of the Wanderer."

Stephen nudged him as if to say: "You see! Only an angel knows such things."

"Stephen," he whispered.

"Yes?"

"I'm not afraid anymore. Of leaving the castle. Not even of the forest!"

"Aren't you, John?"

"Because I'm not alone?"

"I told you we were safe with our angel!"

"I don't mean the angel." He made a pillow of Stephen's shoulder, and the scent of dogs and hay-lofts effaced Ruth's galangal.

"Go to sleep, little brother. Dream about London — and the Holy Land."

But fear returned to John before he could dream. At an hour with the feel of midnight, chill and misty and hushed of owls, he was roused by the blast of a horn and a simultaneous shriek like that of a hundred otters caught in a mill-wheel. The sounds seemed to come from a distance and yet were harsh enough to make him throw up his hands to his ears.

"Hunters have found a Mandrake!" cried Stephen, sitting up in the nest. "It's a moonless night, and it must be just after twelve. That's when they hunt, you know. They blow on a horn to muffle the shriek. Let's see what they've caught."

But John was not eager to leave the tree. "If they've killed a Mandrake, they won't want to share it. Besides, they might be brigands."

Ruth had also been roused by the shriek. "John is right," she said. "You shouldn't want to see such a horrible sight. A baby torn from the earth!"

"I'll stay and keep Ruth company," said John, but Stephen hauled him out of the nest and sent him slipping and scraping down the trunk.

"But we can't leave Ruth alone!" he groaned, picking himself up from a bed of acorns.

"Angels don't need protection. Hurry now, or we'll miss the hunters."

They found the Mandrake hunters across the road and deep among the trees, a pair of rough woodsmen, father and son to judge from their height, build, and flaxen hair, though the elder was as bent and brown as a much-used sickle, and his son wore a patch over one of his eyes. The woodsmen were contemplating a dead Mandrake the size and shape of a new-born baby, except for the dirt-trailing tendrils, the outsized genitals, and the greenish tangle of hair which had grown above ground with purple, bell-shaped flowers. The pathetic body twitched like a hatcheted chicken. Dead at its side and bound to it by a rope lay a dog with bloody ears.

Though the night was moonless and the great stars, Arcturus and Sirius, were veiled by the mist of the forest, one of the hunters carried a lantern, and John saw the Mandrake, the dog, and the blood in an eerie, flickering light which made him remember Lucifer's fall to Hell and wonder if he and Stephen had fallen after him.

One of the woodsmen saw them. "Might have gotten yourselves killed, both of you," he scolded, digging beeswax out of his ears with his little finger. "Laid out like that old hound with busted eardrums." He removed a long-bladed knife from his tunic and under his father's direction — "no, no, clean and quick . . . cut it, don't bruise it" — sliced the Mandrake into little rootlike portions, resinous rather than bloody, which he wrapped in strips of muslin and placed carefully in a sharkskin pouch.

"One less of the devils," muttered the father, unbending himself to a rake instead of a sickle. "Another week and it'd have climbed right out of the ground. Joined its folk in the warrens."

"A Richard's ransom in aphro—aphro*disiacs!*" stuttered the son, completing the word with a flourish of triumph. The market for Mandrake roots was lucrative and inexhaustible: aging barons deserted by sexual powers; lovers whose love was unrequited. From

Biblical times, the times of Jacob and Leah, the root had been recognized as the one infallible aphrodisiac. Yes, a Richard's ransom was hardly an overstatement. A man would pay gold and silver, land, and livestock, to win his love or resurrect his lust.

When the woodsmen had finished their grisly dissection, the son smiled at the boys and offered them a fragment the size of a small pea. "You fellows put this in a girl's gruel, and she'll climb all over you."

"He doesn't need it," said John, intercepting the gift. "Girls climb over him as it is. Like ants on a crock of sugar!"

"But you need it, eh?" laughed the son, winking his single eye at John. One-eyed serfs were common in France and England, and most of them had lost their eyes to angry masters and not in fights. Perhaps the young woodsman had not been prompt to deliver firewood for the hearth in a great hall. "Now you'll be the crock. But where's the sugar?"

"He'll have it," said Stephen, noticing John's embarrassment. "Sugar enough for a nest! Give him a year or two. He's only twelve." Then he pointed to the carcass of the dog. "Did you have to use a greyhound? Couldn't you have done it yourselves? After all, you had the wax in your ears."

"Everyone knows a dog gives a sharper jerk. Gets the whole Mandrake at once. Like pulling a tooth, root and all. Besides, he was an old dog. Not many more years in his bones. We can buy a whole kennel with what we make from the root."

When the men had departed, talking volubly about the sale of their treasure at the next fair, and how they would spend their money in secret and keep their lord from his customary third, the boys buried the dog.

"I wish they had put beeswax in his ears too," said Stephen bitterly. "And see where they whipped him to make him jump!"

"Beeswax doesn't help a dog," said John. "At least I read that in a bestiary. His ears are so keen that the shriek penetrates the wax and kills him anyway."

"It's no wonder the Mandrakes eat us. The way we drag their babies from the ground and cut them up! If it weren't for my parents, I could pity the poor little brutes. Now, a lot of dirty old men will strut like coxcombs and chase after kitchen wenches."

"I suppose," said John, who had furtively buried the fragment of Mandrake with the dog, "the question is, who started eating whom first." Then he clutched Stephen's hand and said: "I think I'm going to be sick."

"No, you're not," said Stephen, steadying John with his arm. "We're going back to the tree and get some sleep."

But Stephen was trembling too; John could feel the tremors in his arm. He's sad for the dog, he thought. I *won't* be sick. It would only make him sadder.

Ruth was waiting for them with a look which they could not read in the misted light of the stars.

"We're sorry we left you so long," said Stephen,

"but the hunters had just killed a Mandrake, and. . . ."

"I don't want to hear about it."

"Mandrakes can't climb trees, can they?" asked John. "The parents might be about, you know. Like that other time."

"Of course they can climb trees," said Stephen, who was very knowledgeable about the woods and improvised what he did not know. "They *are* trees, in a way. Roots at least."

"Do you think they suspect we're up here? They can't see us, but can they sniff us out?"

"I wish you two would stop talking about Mandrakes," snapped Ruth. "You would think they surrounded us, when everyone knows the poor creatures are almost extinct."

"Stephen's parents were killed by Mandrakes," said John sharply. He would have liked to slap the girl. She had a genius for interruptions or improprieties. It was proper and generous for Stephen to express compassion for a Mandrake baby, but unforgivable for this ignorant girl to sympathize with the whole murderous race. Her ethereal origins now seemed about as likely to him as an angel dancing on the head of a pin, a possibility which, to John's secret amusement, his Abbot had often debated with utmost seriousness.

Ruth gave a cry. "I didn't know."

"How could you?" said Stephen. "They crept out of the forest one night when I was gone. The females are also dangerous — the young ones who pass for human and come to live in the towns. The males can't do it;

they're much too hairy right from the start, and — well, *you* know. Too well endowed. But the little girls look human, at least on the outside. Inside, it's a different matter — resin instead of blood; brown skeletons which're — what would you call them, John?"

"Fibrous."

Ruth listened in silence and shrank herself into a little ball. Like a diadem spider, thought John, with brilliant gold patterns. Drawing in her legs and looking half her size.

"Tell her about them, John," said Stephen, who was getting breathless from such a long speech. "You know the whole story." And then to Ruth: "He knows everything. French, English, Latin. All our kings and queens from Arthur down to bad old King John. Even those naughty pagan goddesses who went about naked and married their brothers."

John was delighted to continue the history. He liked to deliver lectures, but nobody except Stephen ever listened to him.

"In the old days, before the Crusades," said John, who warmed to his tale like a traveling storyteller, "in the old days the Mandrakes lived in the forest, and they were so dirty and hairy that you could never mistake them for human. They weren't particular about their diet. They liked any meat — animal or human — and they trapped hunters in nets and roasted them over hot coals and then strewed their bones on the ground as we do with drumsticks at Michaelmas." Here, like a skilled jongleur, he paused and looked at

Ruth to gauge the effect of his tale. The sight of her reassured him. If she pressed any harder against the edge of the nest, she would roll from the tree. "But one day a little Mandrake girl wandered out of the forest, and a simple blacksmith took her for a lost human child, naked and dirty from the woods, and took her into his family. The child grew plump and beautiful, the man and his wife grew peaked, and everyone said how generous it was for a poor blacksmith to give his choicest food — and there wasn't much food that winter for anyone — to a foundling. But in the summer the girl was run down and killed by a wagon loaded with hay. The townspeople were all ready to garrot the driver — until they noticed that the girl's blood was a mixture of normal red fluid and thick, viscous resin."

"What does 'viscous' mean?" interrupted Stephen.

"Gluey. Like that stuff that comes out of a spider when she's spinning her web. Thus, it was learned that Mandrakes are vampires as well as cannibals, and that the more they feed on humans, the less resinous their blood becomes, until the resin is almost replaced, though their bones never do turn white. But they have to keep on feeding or else their blood will revert.

"Well, the Mandrakes heard about the girl — from a runaway thief, no doubt, before they ate him — and how she had 'passed' until the accident. They decided to send some more of their girls into the villages, where life was easier than in the forest. Some of the Mandrakes slipped into houses at night and left their babies, well-scrubbed of course, in exchange for humans, which they carried off into the woods for you can imagine what foul purposes. The next morning the family would think that the fairies had brought them a changeling, and everyone knows that if you disown a fairy's child, you'll have bad luck for the rest of your life. It was a long time before the plan of the Mandrakes became generally known around the forest. Now, whenever a mother finds a strange baby in her crib, or a new child wanders into town, it's usually stuck with a knife. If resin flows out, the child is suffocated and burned. Still, an occasional Mandrake does manage to pass.

"You see, they aren't at all like the Crusaders in the last century who became vampires when they marched through Hungary — the Hungarian campfollowers, remember, gave them the sickness, and then the Crusaders brought it back to England. They had to break the skin to get at your blood, and they had a cadaverous look about them before they fed, and then they grew pink and bloated. It was no problem to recognize and burn them. But the Mandrake girls, by pressing their lips against your skin, can draw blood right through the pores, and the horrible thing is that they don't look like vampires and sometimes they don't even know what they are or how they were born from a seed in the ground. They feed in a kind of dream and forget everything the next morning."

"I think it's monstrous," said Ruth.

"They are, aren't they?" agreed John happily, satisfied that his story had been a success.

"Not *them*. I mean sticking babies with knives."

"But how else can you tell them from roots? It's because a few people are sentimental like you that Mandrakes still manage to pass."

"Frankly," said Ruth, "I don't think Mandrakes pass at all. I think they keep to themselves in the forest and eat venison and berries and *not* hunters. Now go to sleep. From what you've told me, it's a long way to London. We all need some rest."

"Good night," said Stephen.

"Sweet dreams," said Ruth.

III

The next morning, the sun was a Saracen shield in the sky — Saladin's Shield, a Crusader would have said — and the forest twinkled with paths of sunlight and small white birds which spun in the air or perched on limbs and constantly flickered their tails. Ruth and Stephen stood in the crook of the tree and smiled down at John as he opened his eyes.

"We decided to let you sleep." said Stephen. "You grunted like a boar when I first shook you. So we followed a wagtail to find some breakfast."

"And found you some wild strawberries," said Ruth, her lips becomingly red from the fruit. She gave him a deep, brimming bowl. "I wove it from sedges." For one who professed an ignorance of the forest, she possessed some remarkable skills.

Once on the ground, they finished their breakfast with three-cornered, burry beechnuts, which required some skillful pounding and deft fingers to extract the kernels; and Ruth, appropriating Stephen's beer, took such a generous swallow that she drained the flask.

"To wash down the beechnuts," she explained.

"I don't know why the pigs like them so much," said Stephen. "They're not worth the trouble of shelling."

"The pigs don't shell them," reminded the practical John.

"Anyway," continued Stephen, "we hadn't much choice in this part of the forest. We found a stream though." Hoisting the pouch which held their remnants of food and their few extra garments, he said: "Ruth, get your bundle and let's take a swim."

"I hid it," she reminded him, almost snappishly. "There may be thieves about. I'll get it after we swim."

All that mystery about a crucifix, thought John. As if she suspected Stephen and me of being brigands. And after she drank our beer!

The stream idled instead of gushed, and pepper-wort, shaped like four-leafed clovers, grew in the quiet waters along the banks. Stephen, who took a monthly bath in a tub with the stable hands while the daughters of villeins doused him with water, hurried to pull his tunic over his head. He was justly proud of his body and had once remarked to John, "The less I wear, the better I look. In a gentleman's clothes like yours, I'd still be a yokel. But naked——! Even gentlewomen seem to stare."

But John was quick to restore the proprieties. In the presence of Ruth, he had no intention of showing his thin, white body, or allowing Stephen to show his radiant nakedness.

"You can swim first," he said to her. "Stephen and I will wait in the woods."

"No," she laughed. "You go first. Stephen is already down to his breechclout, and *that* is about to fall. But I won't be far away."

"You won't peep, will you?" John called after her, but Ruth, striding into the forest as if she had a destination, did not answer him.

The stream was chilly in spite of the Saracen sun. John huddled among the pepperwort, the water as high as his knees, till Stephen drenched him with a monumental splash, and then they frolicked among the plants and into the current and scraped each other's backs with sand scooped from the bottom and, as far as John was concerned, Ruth and the road to London could wait till the Second Coming!

When they climbed at last on the bank, they rolled in the grass to dry their bodies. Stephen, an expert wrestler, surprised John with what he called his amphisbaena grip; his arms snaked around John's body like the ends of the two-headed serpent and flattened him on the ground.

"I'm holding you for ransom," he cried, perched on John's chest like the seasprite Dylan astride a dolphin. "Six flagons of beer with roasted malt!"

"I promise —" John began, and freed himself with such a burst of strength that Stephen sprawled in the grass beneath the lesser but hardly less insistent weight of John. "I promise you sixteen licks with an abbot's rod!"

Stephen was not disgruntled. "By Robin's bow," he cried, "you've learned all my tricks!"

"I guess we had better dress," said John, releasing his friend to avoid another reversal. "Ruth will want to swim too. I hope she didn't peep," he added, looking askance at some furiously agitated ferns beyond the grassy bank. To his great relief, they disgorged a white wagtail and not a girl. Still, something had frightened the bird.

"What do you think she would see?" laughed Stephen.

"You," said John, eying his friend with an admiration which was more wistful than envious. Stephen was a boy with a man's body, "roseate-brown from toe to crown," to quote a popular song, and comely enough to tempt an angel. When he shook his wet hair, a great armful of daffodils seemed to bestrew his head. A marriage of beauty and strength, thought John. For the hundredth time he marveled that such a boy could have chosen him for a brother; actually chosen, when they had no bond of blood, nor even of race. He peered down at himself and wished for his clothes. At the castle he never bathed in the tub with his father's friends: only with Stephen, sometimes, in the stream of the old mill-wheel, or alone in the heath from his own little bucket (even in the castle, he had no private room, but slept with the rancid sons of his father's knights).

But Stephen said: "You know, John, you're not so skinny now. You've started to fill out. The bones are there. The strength too, as you just proved. All you need is a little more meat. You'll be a man before you know it."

"Next year?" asked John, though such a prospect seemed as far from his grasp as a fiery-plumaged phoenix. "You were a man at thirteen."

"Ten. But I'm different. I'm a villein. We grow fast. With you, I'd say two or possibly three more years. Then we can wench together for sure."

"Who would want me when she could have you?"

Stephen led him to the bank of the stream. "Look," he said, and pointed to their reflections in a space of clear water between the pepperworts: the bright and the dark, side by side; the two faces of the moon. "I have muscles, yes. But you have brains. They show in your face."

"I don't like my face. I won't even look in those glass mirrors they bring back from the Holy Land. I always look startled."

"Not as much as you did. Why, just since we left the castle, I've seen a change. Yesterday, when you faced down the Knight Templar, I was ready to wet my breechclout! But you never batted an eye. And you looked so *wise*. One day you'll have my muscles, but you can bet a brace of pheasants I'll never have your brains. Come on now, let's give Ruth a chance."

At Stephen's insistence — and he had to insist vigorously — they bundled their tunics and wore only their breechclouts, the shapeless strip of cloth which every man, whether priest, baron, or peasant, twisted around his loins. Now they would look like field hands stripped for a hot day's work, and John's fine tunic would not arouse suspicion or tempt thieves.

"But my shoulders," John began, "they're so white."

"They'll brown in the sun on the way to London," he said, and then: "RUTH, you can take your swim!"

He had to repeat her name before she answered in a thin, distant voice: "Yes, Stephen?"

"You can swim now. You'll have the stream to yourself." To John he smiled. "She took you seriously about not peeping. But you know, John, *we* didn't promise."

"You'd spy on an angel?"

Stephen slapped his back. "Now who's calling her an angel? No, I wouldn't spy. I'd just *think* about it. I've always wondered if angels are built like girls. Let's do a bit of exploring while she bathes. I could eat another breakfast after that swim. But we mustn't stray too far from the stream."

Beyond a coppice of young beeches, Stephen discovered a cluster of slender stalks with fragrant, wispy leaves. "Fennels. Good for the fever you catch in London. We might pick a few, roots and all."

But John, thinking of Mandrakes, had no use for roots and followed his nose to a bed of mint. "This is what your mother used to sweeten her gowns, isn't it?"

"Yes, and it's also good to eat." They knelt in the moist soil to pluck and chew the leaves, whose sweetly burning juices left them hoarse and breathless, as if they had gulped a heady muscatel.

But where was the stream, the road, the oak in which they had slept?

"The trees all look the same," said Stephen, "but there, that old beech. Haven't we seen it before? And there, the torn ground —"

They had wandered, it seemed, to the place of the Mandrake hunt. The hole remained in the earth, disturbingly human-shaped, with branching clefts from which the limbs had been wrenched by the hapless dog.

"Let's get away from here," said John, as nausea slapped him like the foul air of a *garderobe*.

"Wait," said Stephen. "There's a second hole. It's — it's where we buried the dog. *God's Bowels!* The dirty Infidels have dug him up and —"

Around the hole they saw a litter of bones . . . skull . . . femur . . . pelvis . . . stripped of their meat and scattered carelessly through the grass.

"Stephen," said John, seizing his friend's hand. "I

111

know how you feel. It was cruel of them to eat the dog. But we've got to get away from here. They'll take us for the hunters!"

Something had waited for them.

At first it looked like a tree. No, a corpse exhumed from a grave with roots entwining its limbs. It wheezed; lurched; moved, swaying, toward them. It was bleached to the color of a beechnut trunk — at least, those parts of the skin (or was it bark?) which showed through the greenish forest of hair (or rootlets?). Red eyes burned in black hollows (tiny fire-dragons peering from caves, thought John). The mouth seemed a single hairlip until it split into a grin which revealed triangular teeth like those of a shark: to crush, tear, shred.

"Run!" screamed John, tugging at his friend, but proud Stephen had chosen to fight.

"Dog-eater!" He charged the Mandrake and used his head for a ram.

The creature buckled like a rotten door but flung out its limbs and enveloped Stephen into its fall; fallen, it seemed a vegetable octopus, lashing viny tentacles around its prey.

Unlike Stephen, John grew cold with anger instead of hot; blue instead of flushed; as if he had plunged in a river through broken ice. First he was stunned. Then the frost-caves of his brain functioned with crystalline clarity. He knew that he was young and relatively weak; against that bark-tough skin, his naked fists would beat in vain. A blind, weaponless charge would not avail his friend. He fell to his knees and mole-like clawed the ground. Pebbles. Pine cones. Beechnuts. Pretty, pretty, useless. Then, a stone, large and jagged. With raw, bleeding hands, he wrestled the earth for his desperately needed weapon and, without regaining his feet, lunged at the fallen Mandrake. The fibrous skull cracked and splintered sickeningly beneath the stone and spewed him with resin and green vegetable matter like a cabbage crushed by a millstone.

"Stephen!" he cried, but the answer hissed above him, shrill with loathing:

"Human!"

Multitudinous fingers caught and bound him with coils of wild grapevine and dragged him, together with Stephen, over the bruising earth.

The Mandrake warrens were not so much habitations as lightless catacombs for avoiding men and animals. No one knew if the creatures had built them or found, enlarged, and connected natural caves and covered the floors with straw. John was painfully conscious as his thin body, little protected by the shreds of his breechclout, lurched and scraped down a tortuous passage like the throat of a dragon. His captors, he guessed, could see in the dark, but only the scraping of Stephen's body told him that he had not been separated from his friend.

"Mother of God," he breathed, "let him stay unconscious!"

For a long time he had to judge their passage from

room to room by the sudden absence of straw which marked a doorway. Finally, a dim, capricious light announced their approach to a fire; a council chamber perhaps; the end of the brutal journey.

The room of the fire was a round, spacious chamber where Mandrake females were silently engaged in piling chunks of peat on a bed of coals. Neither roots nor branches were used as fuel, John saw, since that which began as a root did not use wood for any purpose. Wryly he wondered how the Mandrakes would feel if they knew that the fuel they burned had once been vegetation.

Their captors dumped them as men might deposit logs beside a hearth, and joined the women in feeding the fire. John was tightly trussed, his feet crossed, his hands behind his back, but he rolled his body to lie on his side and look at Stephen's face. His friend's cheeks were scratched; his forehead was blue with a large bruise; and the daffodils of his hair were wilted with blood and cobwebs.

"Stephen, Stephen, what have they done to you?" he whispered, biting his lip to stifle the threat of tears. His hero, fallen, moved him to tenderness transcending worship. For once he had to be strong for Stephen. He had to think of escape.

He examined the room. There were neither beds nor pallets. Apparently the Mandrakes slept in the smaller rooms and used their council chamber as a baron used his hall. It was here that they met to talk and feast. The earthen walls were blackened from

114

many fires. Bones littered the straw, together with teeth, fur, and hair; inedible items. The stench of the refuse was overpowering and, coupled with that of excrement and urine, almost turned John's stomach. He fought nausea by wondering how his fastidious Abbot would have faced the situation: identified himself, no doubt, with Hercules in the Augean stables or Christ amid the corruptions of the Temple.

Then, across the room, he saw the crucifix. Yes, it was unmistakable, a huge stone cross. Latin, with arms of unequal length, and set in an alcove shaped like an apse. Turtle-backed stones served as seats. Between the seats the ground had been packed and brushed by the knees of suppliants. The place was clearly a chapel, and John remembered the tale — a myth, he had always supposed — that after the Christians had come to England with Augustine, a priest had visited the Mandrakes in their warrens. Once they had eaten him, they had reconsidered his words and adopted Christianity.

"Bantling-killer!"

A Mandrake slouched above him, exuding a smell of tarns stagnant with scum. His voice was guttural and at first unintelligible. Bantling-killer. Of course. *Baby*-killer. The creature was speaking an early form of English. He went on to curse all athelings in their byrnies — knights in their mail — and to wish that the whale-road would swallow the last of them as they sailed to their wars in ring-prowed ships of wood. Then, having blasted John's people, he became specific and accused John and Stephen of having killed the bantling with their dog. *His* bantling, he growled, grown from his own seed. Though the Mandrakes copulated like men and animals, John gathered that their females gave birth to objects resembling acorns which they planted in the ground and nurtured into roots. If allowed by hunters to reach maturity, the roots burst from the ground like a turtle out of an egg, and their mothers bundled them into the warrens to join the tribe — hence, the word "bantling" from "bantle" or "bundle."

"No," John shook his head. "No. We did not kill your baby. Your bantling. It was hunters who killed him!"

The creature grinned. A grin, it seemed, was a Mandrake's one expression; anger or pleasure provoked the same bared teeth. Otherwise, he looked as vacant as a cabbage.

"Hunters," he said. "You."

The crowded room had grown as hot as the kitchen before a feast in a castle, but the figures tending the fire, hunched as if with the weight of dirt, toil, and time, seemed impervious to the heat. They had obviously built the fire to cook their dinner, and now they began to sharpen stakes on weathered stones. Even the stakes were tin instead of wood.

The whir of the flames must have alerted the young Mandrakes in the adjacent chambers. They trooped into the room and gathered, gesticulating, around the two captives. They had not yet lapsed into the tired shuffle of their elders; they looked both energetic and intelligent. Life in the forest, it seemed, slowly stultified quick minds and supple bodies. It was not surprising that the weary elders, however they hated men, should try to pass their daughters into the villages.

The girls John saw, except for one, appeared to be adolescents, but hair had already forested their arms and thickened their lips. The one exception, a child of perhaps four, twinkled a wistful prettiness through her grime. Her eyes had not yet reddened and sunken into their sockets; her mouth was the color of wild raspberries. She could still have passed.

The children seemed to have come from the midst of a game. Dice, it appeared, from the small white objects they rattled, a little like the whale-bone cubes which delighted the knights in John's castle. But the dice of the Mandrake children were not so much cubes as irregular, bony lumps scratched with figures. The Greeks, John recalled from the Abbot's lectures, had used the knucklebones of sheep and other animals in place of cubes.

But the Mandrake children had found a livelier game. They stripped John and Stephen of their breechclouts and began to prod their flesh with fingers like sharp carrots and taunt them for the inadequacy of human loins. The Mandrake boys, naked like their parents, possessed enormous genitals; hence, the potency of the murdered, fragmented roots as aphrodisiacs. Stephen stirred fitfully but to John's relief did not awake to find himself the object of ridicule. With ex-

117

cellent reason, he had always taken pride in the badge of his manhood, and to find himself surpassed and taunted by boys of eight and nine would have hurt him more than blows. Only the girl of four, staring reproachfully at her friends, took no part in the game.

A church bell chimed, eerily, impossibly it seemed to John in such a place, and a hush enthralled the room. An aged Mandrake, rather like a tree smothered by moss, hobbled among the silenced children and paused between John and Stephen. Examining. Deliberating. Choosing. He chose Stephen. When he tried to stoop, however, his back created like a rusty drawbridge. He will break, thought John. He will never reach the ground. But he reached the ground and gathered Stephen in his mossy arms.

"Bloody Saracen!" shouted John. "Take your hands off my friend!" Stretching prodigiously, he managed to burst the bonds which held his ankles and drive his knee into the Mandrake's groin. The creature gave such a yelp that red-hot pokers seemed to have gouged John's ears. He writhed on the ground and raised his hands to shut out the shriek and the pain. Shadows cobwebbed his brain. When he struggled back to clarity, Stephen lay in the chapel before the crucifix. Looming above him, the aged Mandrake stood like Abraham above Isaac. The other adults, perhaps twenty of them, sat on the turtle-shaped stones, while the children sat near the fire to watch the proceedings from which their elders had barred them. The impression John caught of their faces — brief, fleeting, hazy with smoke and the dim light of the room — was not one of malice or even curiosity, but respect and fear, and the pretty child had turned her back and buried her face in the arms of an older girl.

The officiating Mandrake intoned what seemed to be a prayer and a dedication. John caught words resembling "Father" and "Son" and realized with horror if not surprise that just as the Christian humans burned a Yule log and decked their castles with hawthorn, holly, and mistletoe in honor of Christ, so the Christian Mandrakes were dedicating Stephen to a different conception of the same Christ. First, the offering, then the feast. The same victim would serve both purposes.

He had already burst the grapevines which held his ankles. In spite of his bound hands, he struggled to his feet and reeled toward the chapel. Once, he had killed a Mandrake with cold implacability. Now he had turned to fire: the Greek fire of the East, hurled at ships and flung from walls; asphalt and crude petroleum, sulphur and lime, leaping and licking to the incandescence of Hell. He felt as if stones and Mandrakes must yield before his advance; as if Mary, the Mother of Christ, must descend from the castles of heaven or climb from the sanctuary of his heart and help him deliver his friend.

But the Mandrakes rose in a solid palisade; and, shrunk to a boy of twelve, he hammered his impotent fists against their wood.

"No," he sobbed, falling to his knees. "Me. Not Stephen."

"JOHN."

His name tolled through the room like the clash of a face against an iron helmet. "John, he will be all right." Her flaxen hair, coarsened with dirt and leaves, rioted over her shoulders like tarnished gold coins. She wore her linen robe, but the white cloth had lost its purity to stains and tears. She might have been a fallen angel, and her eyes seemed to smolder with memories of heaven or visions of Hell.

She had entered the room accompanied, not compelled. She was not their captive. She has gained their favor, he thought, by yielding to their lust. But God will forgive her if she saves my friend, and I, John, will serve her until I die. If she saves my friend —

He saw that she held her crucifix; gripped it as if you would have to sever the hand before you could pry her fingers from its gold arms.

One of her companions called to the priest, who stood impassively between his cross of stone and his congregation, and above Stephen. He neither spoke nor gestured, but disapproval boomed in his silence.

Ruth advanced to the fire and held her crucifix in the glow of the flames, which ignited the golden arms to a sun-washed sea, milkily glinting with pearls like Saracen ships, and the Mandrakes gazed on such a rarity as they had never seen with their poor sunken eyes or fancied in their dim vegetable brains. In some pathetic, childlike way, they must have resembled the men of the First Crusade who took Jerusalem from the Seljuk Turks and gazed, for the first time, at the Holy Sepulchre; whatever ignoble motives had led them to Outre-Mer, they were purged for that one transcendent moment of pride and avarice and poised between reverence and exaltation. It was the same with the Mandrakes.

The priest nodded in grudging acquiescence. Ruth approached him through the ranks of the Mandrakes, which parted murmurously like rushes before the advancing slippers of the wind, and placed the crucifix in his hands. His fingers stroked the gold with slow, loving caresses and paused delicately on the little mounds of the pearls. She did not wait to receive his dismissal. Without hesitation and without visible fear, she walked to John and unbound his hands.

"Help me with Stephen," she said. "I have traded the cross for your lives."

Once they had stooped from the shadows of the last cave and risen to face the late morning sun, the Mandrake left them without a look or a gesture, avid, it seemed, to return to the council chamber and the bartered crucifix. In the dark corridors, Stephen had regained consciousness but leaned on Ruth and John and allowed them to guide his steps, their own steps guided by the slow, creaking shuffle of the Mandrake.

"Stephen, are you all right?" John asked.

"Tired," he gasped, stretching his battered limbs in the grass and closing his eyes.

"And you, Ruth?" John looked at her with awe and wonderment and not a little fear. He had witnessed a miracle.

She did not look miraculous as she lay beside Stephen. Once she had seemed to shrink into a spider; now she reminded him of a wet linen tunic, flung to the ground, torn, trampled, forsaken.

"What happened, Ruth?"

"They found me by the bank after my swim. I reached for a stocking and looked up to see — them."

"And —?"

"They laid hands on me. Dragged me toward their warrens. I fought them, but the one who held me was very strong."

"And you thought of the crucifix? How they were Christians and might value it?"

"Yes. You remember, I had hidden it in our tree. I tried to make them understand that I would give them a treasure if they let me go. You know how they talk. Like little children just learning to speak. Words and phrases all run together. But strange, old-fashioned words. I kept shouting, 'Treasure, treasure!' but they didn't understand. Finally, I remembered an old word used by our ancestors. 'Folk-hoarding,' I cried, and 'Crucifix!' and they understood. They're very devout in their way. They grinned, argued, waved their snaky arms. Then they let me go. I led them to the tree. We passed the place where you and Stephen had fought. I saw bits of your breechclouts and knew their friends had captured you. I stopped in my tracks and said I wanted your freedom as well as mine. Otherwise, no exchange. One of them said, 'If crucifix ring-bright. If time —'

"They climbed right after me up the trunk of the tree. The sight of the crucifix as I unwrapped it made them hold their breath. I held it out to them, but they shook their heads. No, they wouldn't touch it. It was for their priest. They seemed to feel their own filth and ugliness might tarnish the gold or lessen the magic. They didn't grin or look vacant anymore. They looked as if they wanted to cry. They turned their backs and let me dress in the robe — and brought me here."

"And they kept their promise."

"Of course. They're Christians, aren't they?"

Her story troubled him. He had heard of many Christians who failed to keep promises; Crusaders, for example, with Greeks or Saracens. "But why —" he began, meaning to ask why the Mandrakes would feel bound by a promise to a hated human girl.

"We can't sit here all day," she interrupted. "They might change their minds, Christian or not. Where is the road?"

Shakily they climbed to their feet, Stephen without help at his own request ("I must get my balance back."), and saw the trees which encircled and encaged them, great sycamores and greater oaks, looking as if they were sentient old kings in an old country, Celt, Roman, and Saxon, watchfully standing guard until the usurping Normans had felt the slow fingers of the land shape them to the lineaments of Britannia,

Britain, England, as the paws and tongue of a bear sculpture her cub into her own small likeness.

"I think," said Stephen, "that the road lies *that* way."

But Stephen was still befuddled by the blows to his head. They walked for a long time and did not come to the road . . . but came to the Manor of Roses.

Part Three: Lady Mary

I

I watched them as they struggled out of the forest, the stalwart boy supported by his friends, the slighter, dark-haired boy and the girl with angel hair. On a sunny morning, you see, I leave the Manor with the first twittering of sparrows and gather the white roses from the hedge which surrounds my estate, or visit the windmill, the first, I believe, in southern England, and watch the millstones, powered no longer by water, grinding grain for the bread of my kitchen. Now, it was afternoon. I had lunched in the shade of a mulberry tree (apricots, bread, and mead), returned to the hedge of roses, and seen the children. I must have gasped at the sight. They stopped and stared at me over the hedge. The girl stiffened and whispered to the boys. It was not a time when children called at strange manor houses. Startled sparrows, they seemed. Not in littleness or frailty, you understand. The girl and the older boy were more than children. It was rather their vulnerability. Something had almost broken them, and they did not know if I were hunter or friend. I had to prove my friendliness as if I were coaxing sparrows to eat from my hand.

"Follow the hedge to the right," I smiled. "You will see the gate. If you've come from the forest, you must be tired and hungry. I can give you food and a place to sleep." I had made a basket of roses out of my arms. I had no fear of thorns, with my gloves of antelope leather; my long, tight sleeves buttoned at the wrist; my wimple and cap; and my blue, ankle-length skirt, brocaded with star-colored fleurs-de-lis and hanging in folds from my low-belted waist. I watched the boys, clad in breechclouts clumsily fashioned from leaves, and envied them a man's freedom to dress and ride where he will (unless he dresses in armor and rides to war).

The youngest, the dark-haired boy, still supporting his friend, addressed me with the courteous French of a gentleman:

"We are not attired for the company of a lady. You

see, we have come from the forest." His face confirmed
the impression of his speech. It is said that Saladin,
England's noblest enemy, had such a face as a boy:
ascetic, scholar, poet. But first and last, I saw his need
and that of his friend, the Saxon lad with the build
of wandering Aengus, the Great Youth, whose kisses
were called his birds. Even the breechclout seemed an
affront to his body. Still, he needed me. His mouth,
though forced to a smile, was tight with fatigue and
hunger, and a wound had raked his forehead. Both
were spider-webbed with scratches.

The girl, though her white gown was stained and
torn, resembled an angel sculptured from ivory and
set in the tympanum of a London cathedral: beautiful, aloof, expressionless. She is tired, I thought. Weariness has drained her face. Later I will read her heart.

I met them at the wicket in the hedge, a gate so
small and low that my son had jumped it in a single
bound when he rode for the Stane and London.

I held out my arms to greet them; my armful of
roses.

They kept their ground, the dark boy straining toward me, the girl away from me, the Saxon drawn
between them.

"I can offer you more than flowers," I said, spilling
the roses.

The Norman said, "My Lady, whom have we the
honor of addressing?"

"I am called the Lady Mary. You have come to the
Manor of Roses."

"I thought," he said, "you might be another Mary. Will you help my friend? He has suffered a blow to his head." But it was the Norman and not his friend I helped. He swayed on his feet, leaned to my strength, and caught my outstretched hand.

"I will soil your gown."

"With the good brown earth? It is the purest of all substances. The mother of roses."

"But you scattered your flowers on the ground."

"I have others." Supporting him with my arm and followed by his friends, I drew him toward the house.

Once, a moat had surrounded the Manor, but after my husband's death I had filled the water with earth and planted mulberry trees, aflutter now with linnets and silvery filamented with the webs of silkworms; the trees formed a smaller ring within the ring of the rose hedge to island but not to isolate my house, which was built of bricks instead of the cold grey stones preferred by the neighboring barons. My husband had offered to build me a manor for my wedding gift.

"Build it of bricks," I had said. "The color of your hair."

"And stoutly," he said. But the high curtain wall with its oaken door, its rows of weathered bricks from a ruined Roman villa, and its narrow embrasures for bowmen to fire their arrows, had somehow a look of having lost its threat, like armor hung on the wall. Gabriel knows, I could not stand a siege with my poor, bedraggled retainers: gardeners, gatemen, cooks, seneschal, stable-boy — thirty in all, without a knight among them. The wasting fever had not been kind to the Manor of Roses.

The gatekeeper moved to help me with the boy. "He will tire you, my Lady."

I shook my head. No burden can equal the ache of emptiness.

Once we had entered the bailey, Sarah the cook, who had slipped out of the kitchen and thrown back her hood to catch some sun, tossed up her ponderous hands — I suspect it required some effort — and squealed, "My Lady, what have you found?"

"Children, what else? Sarah, hurry to the kitchen and prepare a meal such as young boys — young men — like. Pheasant and —"

"I know, I know," she said. "You forget I've sons of my own, who serve you every night!" Sarah, her three sons and her two daughters, were new to the Manor, but she acted as if she had been my nurse since childhood. "I know what young boys like. The beast of the chase and the fowl of the warren. All that flies and all that goes on hooves, and two of everything unless it's as big as a boar!" She waddled ahead of us up the stairs to the door and, laboriously genuflecting, vanished under the lintel with its wooden Madonna cradling the Holy Infant.

"It's a lovely house," said the Saxon boy, in English. "It looks like an abbot's grange."

"A very rich abbot," explained the Norman, fearful no doubt that I had misunderstood his friend's compliment, since poor abbots lived in squalid cottages.

"I meant," stammered the Saxon, "it looks so bright and peaceful, with its Mother and Child, and its —" He waited for his friend to complete his sentence.

"Its two pointed roofs instead of battlements, and real windows instead of slits for archers, with *glass* in the windows! And, Stephen, see the herb garden. Parsley, thyme, bay leaf, marjoram, mace, tarragon—"

"You know a lot about herbs," I said.

"I've read an herbal."

Once in the Manor, I took them to the bath. In all the Weald, I think, in all of England, no other house can claim a fountain for bathing enclosed under the roof. The mouth of a dolphin, hammered from bronze by the artisans of Constantinople, spewed a vigorous streamlet into a basin where Tritons gamboled on varicolored tiles. For baths in the cold of winter, I stuffed the dolphin's mouth and filled the basin with kettles hot from the kitchen.

"Your friend shall bathe first," I said to the boys. All of us now were speaking English. And to her: "Your name is —?"

When the girl was slow to answer, the Saxon said: "Ruth. She is our guardian angel. She rescued us."

"From wild beasts?"

"From Mandrakes."

I shuddered. "They are much in the woods, poor misshapen brutes. They have never harmed me, though. You must tell me later about your escape. Now then, Ruth. You shall have the bath to yourself. After you have bathed, I shall send you clothes, and a perfume made from musk, and . . ."

She looked at me with cool, veiled eyes. "You are very kind." I wanted to say to her: I am more than twice your age, and far less beautiful. Trust me, my dear. Trust me!

I turned to the boys. The Norman, I learned, was John; the Saxon, Stephen. "When Ruth has finished, it will be your turn."

"Thank you, my Lady," said John. "We would like to bathe with a dolphin. But —"

"You would rather eat! What about bread and cheese and pennyroyal tea to hold you till time for supper? Or," I added quickly, "beer instead of tea." Pennyroyal! I had been too much with women.

"Beer," they said in one breath. "But," said John, "my brother has a wound."

"Brother?" I asked, surprised. A Norman gentleman and a Saxon peasant!

"We adopted each other. Have you something for his head?"

"For my stomach," grinned Stephen. "That's where I hurt the most."

"For both," I said.

The hall of my manor house is hot and damp in the summer, and cold in the winter even with pine logs, as big around as a keg of beer, crackling on the hearth. It has always been a room for men: shouting, roistering, warming themselves with mead. For myself, I prefer the solar, the room of many purposes in which

I sleep and dine and weave, and entertain the friends who come infrequently now to visit me. I left the boys in the solar with three loaves of bread, two enormous cheeses, and a flagon of beer, and told them to eat and afterwards to bathe themselves with cloths dipped in camphor and wrap fresh linen around their waists.

"Call me after you've finished."

I had scarcely had time to find a gown for Ruth when I heard John's voice: "Lady Mary, we've finished."

I found them so fragrant with camphor that I overlooked the patches of dirt they had left on their knees and elbows. The bread, cheese, and wine had vanished as if there had been a raid by kitchen elves, denied their nightly tribute of crumbs. I tended the boys' wounds with a paste of fennel and dittany and they yielded themselves to my fingers without embarrassment, sons to a mother, and made me feel as if my hands had rediscovered their purpose.

"It doesn't burn at all," said Stephen. "My father used a poultice of adder's flesh pounded with wood-lice and spiders. But it burned like the devil, and stank."

"Lady Mary's hands are like silk," said John. "That's why it doesn't burn."

The boys began to dress in tunics which had belonged to my son: John in green, with a fawn-colored cape drawn through a ring-brooch and knotted at his shoulder, and *chausses* or stockings to match the cape, and black leather shoes with straps; Stephen in blue, with a pale rose cape and silver *chausses,* but looking with each additional garment as if another chain had shackled him to the wall.

"I wouldn't show myself in the forest like this," he muttered. "I'd be taken for a pheasant and shot on sight."

"It's only for tonight," I said. "Don't you want to look the gallant for Ruth?"

"She's used to me naked. She'll take me for a jester."

"My Lady."

Ruth had entered the room. She was dressed in a crimson gown or *cotte,* caught at the waist by a belt of gilded doeskin but falling around her feet in billows through which the toes of her slippers peeped like small green lizards. She had bound her hair in a moss-green net, and her yellow tresses twinkled like caged fireflies. (Strange, I always thought of her in terms of forest creatures: wild; unknowable; untamable.)

"My Lady, the boys may have their bath. I thank you for sending me so lovely a gown."

"We've had our bath," said Stephen with indignation. "Can't you see we're dressed as gallants?"

"Lady Mary put fennel and dittany on our wounds," said John, "and now they don't hurt any more."

"And we're going to eat," said Stephen.

"Again," said John.

Ruth examined the solar and almost relaxed from her self-containment. "Why, it's lovely," she said, extending her arm to include the whole of the room. "It's all made of sunlight."

"Not entirely," I smiled, pointing to the high,

raftered ceiling with its tie-beam and king-post. "Cobwebs collect unless I keep after Sarah's sons. They have to bring a ladder, you see, and they don't like dusting among the dark crevices. They're afraid of elves."

"But the rest," Ruth said. "There's no darkness anywhere."

The room was kindled with afternoon light from the windows: the fireplace, heaped with logs; a tall-backed chair with square sides and embroidered cushions or bankers; a huge recessed window shaped like an arch and filled with roseate panes of glass from Constantinopole; and, hiding the wooden timbers of the floor, a Saracen carpet of polygons, red, yellow, and white, with a border of stylized Persian letters. My wainscotted walls, however, were purely English, their oaken panels painted the green of leaves and bordered with roses to match the carpet.

Ruth explored the room with the air of a girl familiar with beauty, its shapes and its colors, but not without wonder. She touched my loom with loving recognition and paused at my canopied bed to exclaim: "It's like a silken tent!"

"But the linnets," she said, pointing to the wicker cage which hung beside the bed. "Don't they miss the forest?"

"They are quite content. I feed them sunflower seeds and protect them from stoats and weasels. In return, they sing for me."

"Is it true that a caged linnet changes his song?"

"Yes. His voice softens."
"That's what I mean. The wildness goes."
"Shouldn't it, my dear?"
"I don't know, Lady Mary."

We sat on benches drawn to a wooden table with trestles, John and I across from Ruth and Stephen. My husband and I had been served in the great hall by nimble, soft-toed squires who received the dishes from kitchen menials. After his death, however, I began to dine in the solar instead of the hall. For the last year I had been served by Shadrach, Meshach, and Abednego, the three illegitimate sons of my cook, Sarah. As a rule, I liked to dine without ceremony, chatting with the sons — identical triplets with fiery red hair on their heads and arms, and thus their name: they seemed to have stepped out of a furnace. But tonight, for the sake of my guests, I had ordered Sarah and her two illegitimate daughters, Rahab and Magdalena, to prepare, and her sons to serve, a banquet instead of a supper. The daughters had laid the table with a rich brocade of Saracen knights astride their swift little ponies, and they had placed among the knights, as if it were under siege, a molded castle of sugar, rice-flour, and almond-paste.

After I had said the grace, the sons appeared with lavers, ewers, and napkins and passed them among my guests. Stephen lifted a laver to his mouth and started to drink, but John whispered frantically:

"It isn't soup, it's to wash your hands."

"There'll be other things to drink," I promised.

"I haven't felt this clean since I was baptized!" Stephen laughed, splattering the table with water from his laver.

Both Ruth and John, though neither had eaten from dishes of beaten silver, were fully at ease with knives and spoons; they cut the pheasant and duck before they used their fingers and scooped the fish-and-crab-apple pie with the spoons. But Stephen watched his friends with wry perplexity.

"I never used a knife except to hunt or fish," he sighed. "I'll probably cut off a finger. Then you can see if I'm a Mandrake!"

"We'd know that already," said John. "You'd look like a hedgehog and somebody would have chopped you up a long time ago for aphrodisiacs. You'd have brought a fortune." His gruesome remarks, I gathered, were meant to divert me from the fact that he had furtively dropped his knife, seized a pheasant, and wrestled off a wing. His motive was as obvious as it was generous. He did not wish to shame his friend by his own polished manners.

I laughed heartily for the first time since the death of my son. "Knives were always a nuisance. Spoons too. What are fingers for if not to eat with? So long as you don't bite yourself!" I wrenched a drumstick and thigh from the parent bird and felt the grease, warm and mouthwatering, ooze between my fingers. "Here," I said to Stephen. "Take hold of the thigh and we'll divide the piece." The bone parted, the meat split into decidedly unequal portions. Half of my drumstick accompanied Stephen's thigh.

"It means you're destined for love," I said.

"He's already had it," said John. "Haylofts full of it."

"She doesn't mean that kind," said Stephen, suddenly serious. "She means caring — taking care of — don't you, Lady Mary? I've had that too, of course." He looked at John.

"Then it means you'll always have it."

"I know," he said.

John smiled at Stephen and then at me, happy because the three of us were friends, but silent Ruth continued to cut her meat into snail-sized portions and lift them to her mouth with the fastidiousness of a nun (her fingers, however, made frequent trips).

Shadrach, Meshach, and Abednego scurried between the solar and the kitchen, removing and replenishing, but it looked as if John and Stephen would never satisfy their hunger. With discreet if considerable assistance from Ruth, they downed three pheasants, two ducks, two fish-and-crabapple pies, and four tumblers of mead.

"Leave some for us," hissed Shadrach in Stephen's ear. "This is the *last* bird." Stephen looked surprised, then penitent, and announced himself as full as a tick on the ear of a hound. Shadrach hurried the last bird back to the kitchen.

After the feast the boys told me about their adventures, encouraging rather than interrupting each other with such comments as, "You tell her about the stream with the pepperwort, John," or "Stephen, you're better about the fighting." John talked more because he was more at ease with words; Stephen gestured as much as he talked and sometimes asked John to finish a sentence for him; and Ruth said nothing until the end of the story, when she recounted, quietly, without once meeting my gaze, the episode of her capture and bargain with the Mandrakes. I studied her while she spoke. Shy? Aloof, I would say. Mistrustful. Of me, at least. Simple jealousy was not the explanation. I was hardly a rival for the kind of love she seemed to want from Stephen. No, it was not my beauty which troubled her, but the wisdom which youth supposes to come with age; in a word, my mature perceptions. There was something about her which she did not wish perceived.

"And now for the gifts," I said.

"Gifts?" cried John.

"Yes. The dessert of a feast is the gifts and not the pies."

"But we have nothing to give you."

"You have told me a wondrous and frightening story. No jongleur could have kept me more enthralled. And for you, I have —" I clapped my hands and Shadrach, Meshach, and Abednego appeared with my gifts, some musical instruments which had once belonged to my son. For Ruth, a rebec, a pear-shaped instrument from the East, three-stringed and played with a bow; for the boys, twin nakers or kettledrums which Stephen strapped to his back and John began to pound with soft-headed wooden drumsticks.

Ruth hesitated with her rebec till Stephen turned and said, "Play for us, Ruth! What are you waiting for, a harp?"

Then Ruth joined them, the boys marching round and round the solar, Stephen first, John behind him pounding on the drums and thumping the carpet with his feet, and finally Ruth, playing with evident skill and forgetting to look remote and enigmatic. Shadrach, Meshach, and Abednego had lingered in the doorway, and behind them Sarah appeared with her plump, swarthy daughters. I was not surprised when they started to sing; I was only surprised to find myself joining them in the latest popular song:

Summer is a-comin' in,
Loud sing cuckoo.
Groweth seed and bloweth mead.
And springs the wood anew.
      Sing, cuckoo!

In an hour the three musicians, their audience departed to the kitchen, had exhausted the energies which the meal had revived. Ruth sank in the chair beside the hearth. The boys, thanking me profusely for their gifts, climbed into the window seats. Stephen yawned and began to nod his head. John, in the opposite seat, gave him a warning kick.

"Come," I said to them. "There's a little room over

141

the kitchen which used to belong to my son. The hall was too big, the solar too warm, he felt. I'll show you his room while Ruth prepares for bed. Ruth, we'll fix you a place in the window. You see how the boys are sitting opposite each other. I've only to join the seats with a wooden stool and add a few cushions to make a couch. Or" — and I made the offer, I fear, with visible reluctance — "you may share my own bed under the canopy."

"The window seats will be fine."

I pointed to the Aumbry, a wooden cupboard aswirl with wrought-iron scrollwork, almost like the illuminated page of a psalter. "There's no lock. Open the doors and find yourself a nightdress while I show the boys their room."

My son's room was as small as a chapel in a keep, with one little square of a window, but the bed was wide as well as canopied, and irresistible to the tired boys.

"It's just like yours!" John cried.

"Smaller. But just as soft."

"At home I slept on a bench against the wall, in a room with eight other boys — sons of my father's knights. I got the wall bench because my father owned the castle."

"I slept on straw," said Stephen, touching the mattress, sitting, stretching himself at length, and uttering a huge, grateful sigh. "It's like a nest of puppies. What makes it so soft?"

"Goose-feathers."

"The geese we ate tonight — *their* feathers will stuff a mattress, won't they?"

"Two, I suspect." I fetched them a silk-covered bearskin from a small, crooked cupboard which my son had built at the age of thirteen. "And now I must see to Ruth."

I am not a reticent person, but the sight of the boys — Stephen in bed and sleepily smiling goodnight, John respectfully standing but sneaking an envious glance at his less respectful friend — wrenched me almost to tears. I did not trust myself to say that I was very glad to offer them my son's bed for as long as they chose to stay in the Manor of Roses.

I could only say: "Sleep as late as you like. Sarah can fix you breakfast at any hour."

"You're very kind," said Stephen. "But tomorrow, I think, we must get an early start for London."

"London!" I cried. "But your wounds haven't healed!"

"They were just scratches really, and now you've cured them with your medicine; if we stayed, we might *never* want to go."

"I might never want you to go."

"But don't you see, Lady Mary, we have to fight for Jerusalem."

"You expect to succeed where kings have failed? Frederick Barbarossa? Richard the Lion-Hearted? Two little boys without a weapon between them!"

"We're not little boys," he protested. "I'm a young swain — *fifteen winters old* — and John here is a —

stripling who will grow like a bindweed. Aren't you, John?"

"Grow, anyway," said John without enthusiasm. "But I don't see why we have to leave in the morning."

"Because of Ruth."

"And Ruth is your guardian angel?" I asked with an irony lost on the boy.

"Yes. Already she's saved our lives."

"Has she, Stephen? Has she? Sleep now. We'll talk tomorrow. I want to tell you about my own son."

I returned to the solar heavy of foot. It was well for Ruth that she had changed to a nightdress, joined the window seats with the necessary stool, and retired to bed in a tumble of cushions. Now, she was feigning sleep but forgetting to mimic the slow, deep breaths of the true sleeper. Well, I could question her tomorrow. One thing I knew. She would lead my boys on no unholy Crusade.

A chill in the air awakened me. It was not unusual for a hot summer day to grow wintry at night. I rose, lit a candle, and found additional coverlets for myself and Ruth. Her face seemed afloat in her golden hair; decapitated, somehow; or drowned.

I thought of the boys, shivering in the draft of their glassless window. I had not remembered to draw the canopy of their bed. In my linen nightdress and my pointed satin slippers which, like all the footwear expected of English ladies, cruelly pinched my toes, I passed through the hall and then the kitchen, tiptoed among the pallets of Sarah and her children stretched near the oven, and climbed a staircase whose steepness resembled a ladder.

Lifting aside a coarse leather curtain, I stood in the doorway of my son's room and looked at the boys. They had fallen asleep without extinguishing the pewter lamp which hung from a rod beside their bed. The bearskin covered their chins, and their bodies had met for warmth in the middle of the bed. I leaned above them and started to spread my coverlet. John, who was closer to me, opened his eyes and smiled.

"Mother," he said.

"Mary," I said, sitting on the edge of the bed.

"That's what I meant."

"I'm sorry I woke you."

"I'm glad. You came to bring us a coverlet, didn't you?"

"Yes. Won't we wake your brother?"

His smile broadened; he liked my acceptance of Stephen as his brother and equal. "Not our voices. Only if I got out of bed. Then he would feel me gone. But once he's asleep, he never hears anything, unless it's one of his hounds."

"You're really going tomorrow?"

"I don't want to go. I don't think Stephen does either. It's Ruth's idea. She whispered to him in the solar, when you and I were talking. But I heard her just the same. She said they must get to London. She said it was why she had come, and why she had saved us from the Mandrakes."

"Why won't she trust me, John?"

"I think she's afraid of you. Of what you might guess."

"What is there to guess?"

There was fear in his eyes. He looked at Stephen, asleep, and then at me. "I think that Ruth is a Mandrake. One who has passed."

I flinched. I had thought: thief, adventuress, harlot, carrier of the plague, but nothing so terrible as Mandrake. Though fear was a brand in my chest, I spoke quietly. I did not want to judge her until he had made his case. He might be a too imaginative child, frightened by the forest and now bewildered with sleep. He was only twelve. And yet, from what I had seen, I had thought him singularly rational for his years. Stephen, one might have said, would wake in the night and babble of Mandrake girls. Never John. Not without reason, at least.

"Why do you think that, John?"

His words cascaded like farthings from a purse cut by a pickpocket: swift, confused at times, and yet with a thread of logic which made me share his suspicions. Ruth's mysterious arrival in the Mithraeum. Her vague answers and her claim to forgetfulness. Her lore of the forest. Her shock and disgust when he and Stephen had told her about the Mandrake hunters. Her strangely successful bargain with the crucifix.

"And they kept their word," he said. "Even when they thought Stephen and I had killed one of their

146

babies. It was as if they let us go so that she could *use* us."

"It's true they're Christians," I said. "I've found their stone crosses in the woods around my Manor. They might have felt bound by their word. An oath to a savage, especially a Christian savage, can be a sacred thing. Far more sacred than to some of our own Crusaders, who have sacked the towns of their sworn friends. Ruth may have told you the truth about the crucifix."

"I know," he said. "I know. It's wicked of me to suspect her. She's always been kind to me. She brought me strawberries in the forest once! And Stephen worships her. But I had to tell you, didn't I? She might have passed when she was a small child. Grown up in a village. But someone became suspicious. She fled to the forest. Took shelter in the Mithraeum where Stephen and I found her. You see, if I'm right —"

"We're all in danger. You and Stephen most of all. You have been exposed to her visitations. We shall have to learn the truth before you leave this house."

"You mean we must wound her? But if she passed a long time ago, we would have to cut to the bone."

"We wouldn't so much as scratch her. We would simply confront her with an accusation. Suppose she is a Mandrake. Either she knew already when she first met you or else her people told her in the forest. Told her with pride: 'See, we have let you grow soft and beautiful in the town!' Tomorrow we shall demand proof of her innocence. Innocent, she will offer herself to the knife. The offer alone will suffice. But a true Mandrake will surely refuse such a test, and then we will know her guilt."

"It's rather like trial by combat, isn't it?" he said at last. "God condemns the guilt. Pricks him with conscience until he loses the fight. But this way, there won't be a combat, just a trial. God will make Ruth reveal her guilt or innocence."

"And you and I will be His instruments. Nothing more."

"And if she's guilty?"

"We'll send her into the forest and let her rejoin her people."

"It will break Stephen's heart. There was another girl he loved, you see. He lost her to the Plague."

"It will save his life. Save him from Ruth — and from going to London. Without his angel, do you think he'll still persist in his foolish crusade? He will stay here with you and me. The Manor of Roses has need of two fine youths."

"You won't make him a servant because he's a villein? His ancestors were Saxon earls when mine were pirates."

"Mine were pirates too. Blood-thirsty ones, at that. No, you and Stephen shall both be my sons. You adopted him. Why shouldn't I?"

"You know," he said, "when you first spoke to us at the hedge — after we had come from the forest — you said we'd come to the Manor of Roses. At first

I thought you meant the *manner* of roses. Without the capitals."

"Did you, John?"

"Yes. And it's quite true. Of the house, I mean, and you. The manner of roses."

"But I have thorns to protect the ones I love. Ruth will feel them tomorrow." I knelt beside him and touched my lips to his cheek. It was not as if I were kissing him for the first time, but had kissed him every night for — how many years? — the years of my son when he rode to London.

"You're crying," he said.

"It's the smoke from the lamp. It has stung my eyes."

He clung to my neck, no longer a boy; a small child I could almost feed at my breast.

"I like your hair when it's loose," he said. "It's like a halo that comes all the way to your shoulders."

He fell asleep in my arms.

II

I woke to the strident twittering of sparrows. Their little shapes flickered against the window panes, and for once I regretted the glass. I would have liked them to flood the room with their unmelodious chirpings and share in my four-walled, raftered safety. Minikin beings, they reveled in the sun, noisily, valiantly, yet prey to eagle and hawk from the wilderness of sky, and the more they piped defiance, the more they invited death.

But other sparrows were not beyond my help.

I rose and dressed without assistance. I did not call Sarah's daughters to comb my hair and exclaim, "But it's like black samite!" and fasten the sleeves above my wrists and burden my fingers with jade and tourmaline. I did not wish to awaken Ruth. I dreaded the confrontation.

Encased from the tip of my toes to the crest of my hair, amber and green in wimple, robe, gloves, stockings, and slippers, I walked into the courtyard and sat on a bench among my herbs, lulled by the soft scent of lavender, but not from my hesitations; piqued by the sharp pungency of tarragon, but not to pride in what I must ask of Ruth.

The sun was as high as a bell-tower before the sounds from the solar told me that the children had waked and met. Ruth and Stephen were belaboring John when I entered the room. Stephen looked liberated in his breechclout, and Ruth disported herself in his green tunic, the one he had worn reluctantly to my feast, but without the *chausses* or the cape. They were telling John that he ought to follow their example and dress for the woods.

"You're white as a sheep this morning," chided Stephen. "Your shoulders need the sun."

John, engulfed by his cape and tunic, might have been ten instead of twelve. I pitied the child. He would have to side with me against his friends. He returned my smile with a slight nod of his head, as if to say, "It must be now."

Stephen's voice was husky with gratitude: "Lady Mary, we must leave you and make our way to London. You've fed us and given us a roof, and we won't forget you. In a dark forest, you have been our candle. Your gifts — the drums and rebec — will help us to earn our passage to the Holy Land."

"Knights and abbots will throw you pennies," I said. "Robbers will steal them. It will take you a long time to earn your passage."

"But that's why we have to go! To start earning. And when we come back this way, we'll bring you a Saracen shield to hang above your hearth." He kissed my hand with a rough, impulsive tenderness. An aura of camphor wreathed him from yesterday's bath. He had combed his hair in a fringe across his forehead, like jonquils above his bluer-than-larkspur eyes. I thought how the work of the comb would soon be spoiled; the petals wilted by the great forest, tangled with cobwebs, matted perhaps with blood.

"I think you should know the nature of your company."

His eyes widened into a question. The innocence of them almost shook my resolve. "John? But he's my friend! If you mean he's very young, you ought to have seen him fight the Mandrakes."

"Ruth."

Ruth is an angel." He made the statement as one might say, "I believe in God."

"You want her to be an angel. But is she, Stephen? Ask her."

153

He turned to Ruth for confirmation. "You said you came from the sky, didn't you?"

"I said I didn't remember." She stared at the Persian carpet and seemed to be counting the polygons or reading the cryptic letters woven into the border.

"But you said you remembered falling a great distance."

"There are other places to fall than out of the sky."

John spoke at last. "But you remembered things." His voice seemed disembodied. It might have come from the vault of a deep Mithraeum. "About the forest. Where to find wild strawberries. How to weave a cup out of rushes. How to escape from the Mandrakes."

"Ruth," I said. "Tell them who you are. Tell me. We want to know."

She began to tremble. "I don't know. I don't know." I was ready to pity her when she told the truth.

I walked to the Aumbry with slow, deliberate steps. In spite of my silken slippers, I placed each foot as if I were crushing a mite which threatened my roses. I opened the doors, knelt, and reached to the lowest shelf for a Saracen poniard, its ivory hilt emblazoned with sapphires in the shape of a running gazelle. The damascene blade was very sharp: steel inlaid with threads of silver.

There was steel in my voice as I said, "You are not to leave my house till I know who you are. I accepted you as a guest and friend. Now I have reason to believe that you are dangerous. To the boys, if not to me."

"You would harm me, Lady Mary?" She shrank from the light of the window and joined the shadows near the hearth. I half expected her to dwindle into a spider and scuttle to safety among the dark rafters.

"I would ask you to undergo a test."

She said: "You think I am a Mandrake."

"I think you must show us that you are not a Mandrake." I walked toward her with the poniard. "My husband killed the Saracen who owned this blade. Wrestled him for it. Drove it into his heart. You see, the point is familiar with blood. It will know what to do."

"Lady Mary!" It was Stephen who stepped between us; charged, I should say, like an angry stag, and almost took the blade in his chest. "What are you saying, Lady Mary?"

"Ask her," I cried. "Ask her! Why does she fear the knife? Because it will prove her guilt!"

He struck my hand and the poniard fell to the floor. He gripped my shoulders. "Witch! You have blasphemed an angel!"

Anger had drained me; indignation; doubts. I drooped in his punishing hands. I wanted to sleep.

John awoke from his torpor and beat on his friend with desperate fists. "It's true, it's true! You must let her go!"

Stephen unleashed a kick like a javelin hurled from an arblast. I forgot the poniard; forgot to watch the girl. All I could see was John as he struck the doors of the Aumbry and sank, winded and groaning to the floor. Twisting from Stephen's fingers, I knelt to the wounded boy and took him in my arms.

"I'm not hurt," he gasped. "But Ruth . . . the poniard . . . "

I saw the flash of light on the blade in Ruth's hand. Stephen swayed on his feet, a stag no longer: a bear chained in a bit, baited by some, fed by others — how can he tell his tormentors from his friends? Wildly he stared from the boy he had hurt to the girl he had championed. Ruth walked toward me with soundless feet and eyes as cold as hornstones under a stream. She might have been dead.

The poniard flashed between us. I threw up my hands for defense: of myself and John. She brought the blade down sharply against her own hand, the mount of the balm below her thumb. I heard — I actually heard — the splitting of flesh, the rasp of metal on bone. The blade must have cut through half of her hand before it lodged in the bone, and then she withdrew it without a cry, with a sharp, quick jerk, like a fisherman removing a hook, and stretched her fingers to display her wound. The flesh parted to reveal white bone, and crimson blood, not in the least resinous, swelled to fill the part. She smiled at me with triumph but without malice, a young girl who had vindicated herself before an accuser more than twice her years.

"Did you think I mean to hurt you?" she said almost

playfully and then, seeing her blood as it reddened the carpet, winced and dropped the poniard.

Stephen steadied her into the chair by the hearth and pressed her palm to staunch the flow.

"You are an evil woman," he glared at me. "Your beauty is a lie. It hides an old heart."

"Both of your friends are in pain," I said. "It isn't a time for curses."

He looked at John in my arms and stiffened as if he would drop Ruth's hand and come to his friend.

"No. Stay with Ruth." I helped John across the room to a seat in the window; the tinted panes ruddied his pale cheeks. "He will be all right. Ruth is in greater need. Let me tend her, Stephen."

"You shan't touch her."

Ruth spoke for herself. "The pain is very sharp. Can you ease it, Lady Mary?"

I treated the wound with a tincture of opium and powdered rose petals and swaddled her hand with linen. John rose from the window and stood behind me, in silent attendance on Ruth — and in atonement. Stephen, an active boy denied a chance to act, stammered to his friends:

"Forgive me, both of you. It was my Crusade, wasn't it? I brought you to this."

Ruth's face was as white as chalk-rubbed parchment awaiting the quill of a monk. Her smile was illumination. "But you see, Stephen, Lady Mary was right to a point. I am no more an angel than you are. Less, in fact. You're a dreamer. I'm a liar. I've lied to

you from the start, as Lady Mary guessed. That's why
I couldn't trust her — because I saw that she couldn't
trust me. My name isn't Ruth; it's Madeleine. I didn't
come from heaven but the Castle of the Boar, three
miles from your own kennels. My father was noble of
birth, brother to the Boar. But he hated the life of a
knight — the hunts, the feasts, the joustings — and
most of all, the Crusades without God's blessing. He
left his brother's castle to live as a scholar in Chichester, above a butcher's shop. He earned his bread
by copying manuscripts or reading the stars. It was
he who taught me my languages — English and Norman French and Latin — and just as if I were a boy,
the lore of the stars, the sea, and the forest. He also
taught me to play the rebec and curtsey and use a
spoon at the table. 'Someday,' he said, 'you will marry
a knight, a gentle one, I hope, if such still exist, and
you have to be able to talk to him about a man's in-
terests, and also delight him with the ways of a woman.
Then he won't ride off to fight in a foolish Crusade,
as most men do because of ignorant wives.' He taught
me well and grew as poor as a Welshman. When he
died of the plague last year, he left me pennies instead
of pounds, and no relatives except my uncle, the Boar,
who despised my father and took me into his castle
only because I was brought to him by an abbot from
Chichester.

"But the Boar was recently widowed, and he had
a taste for women. Soon I began to please him. I think
I must have grown — how shall I say it? — riper,

more womanly. He took me hawking and praised my lore of the forest. I sat beside him at banquets, drank his beer, laughed at his bawdy tales, and almost forgot my Latin. But after a feast one night he followed me to the chapel and said unspeakable things. My own uncle! I hit him with a crucifix from the altar. No one stopped me when I left the castle. No one knew the master was not at his prayers! But where could I go? Where but Chichester. Perhaps the Abbot would give me shelter.

"But John, as I passed near your father's castle I heard a rider behind me. I ducked in a thicket of gorse and tumbled down some stairs into a dark vault. You see, I did have a kind of fall, though not from heaven. I was stiff and tired and scared, and I fell asleep and woke up to hear Stephen proclaiming me an angel and talking about London and the Holy Land. London! Wasn't that better than Chichester? Further away from my uncle? Stephen, I let you think me an angel because I was tired of men and their lust. I had heard stories about you even at the castle — your way with a wench. After I knew you, though, I *wanted* your way. You weren't at all the boy in the stories, but kind and trusting. But I couldn't admit my lie and lose your respect.

"As for the crucifix you found in my hands, I had stolen it from my uncle. He owed me *something*, I felt. I had heard him say it was worth a knight's ransom. I hoped to sell it and buy a seamstress' shop and marry a fine gentleman who brought me stockings to mend.

When I traded it to the Mandrakes, it was just as I said. They kept their promise for the sake of their faith. You see, they were much more honest than I have been."

Stephen was very quiet. I had seen him pressed for words but never for gestures, the outstretched hand, the nod, the smile. I wanted to ease the silence with reassurances and apologies. But Ruth was looking to Stephen; it was he who must speak.

"Now I'm just another wench to you," she said with infinite wistfulness. "I should have told you the truth. Let you have your way. This way, I've nothing at all."

He thought for a long time before he spoke, and the words he found were not an accusation. "I think a part of me never really took you for an angel. At least, not after the first. I'm not good enough to deserve a guardian from heaven. Besides, you stirred me like a girl of flesh and blood. But I wanted a reason for running away. An excuse and a hope. I lacked courage, you see. It's a fearful thing for a villein to leave his master. John's father could have me killed, or cut off my hands and feet. So I lied to myself: An angel had come to guide me! We were both dishonest, Ruth — Madeleine."

"Ruth. That's the name you gave me."

"Ruth, we can still go to London. Without any lies between us." Gestures returned to him; he clasped her shoulders with the deference of a brother (and looked to John: "My arms are not yet filled"). "But Lady

Mary, it was cruel of you to find the truth in such a way."

"She never meant to touch Ruth," said John. "Only to test her. It was things I told Lady Mary that made her suspicious."

"John, John," said Ruth, walking to him and placing her swaddled hand on his arm. "I know you've never liked me. You saw through my tale from the first. You thought I wanted your friend. You were right, of course. I wouldn't trade him for Robin Hood, if Robin were young again and Lord of the forest! But I never wished you ill. You were his chosen brother. How could I love him without loving you? I wanted to say: 'Don't be afraid of losing Stephen to me. It was you he loved first. If I take a part of his heart, it won't be a part that belongs to you. Can't you see, John, that the heart is like the catacombs of the old Christians? You can open a second chamber without closing the first. Trust your friend to have chambers for both of us.' But I said nothing. It would have shown me to be a girl instead of an angel."

"You're coming with us, John?" asked Stephen doubtfully. "I didn't mean to hurt you. It was like the time you stepped on my dog. But you forgave me then."

"There's no reason now why any of you should go," I said.

"There's no reason for us to stay."

"You'll go on a Crusade without a guardian angel?"

"We'll walk to London and then — who knows?

Venice, Baghdad, Cathay! Maybe it was just to run away I wanted, and not to save Jerusalem." He pressed John between his big hands. "You *are* coming, aren't you, brother?"

"No," said John. "No, Stephen. Lady Mary needs me."

"So does Stephen," said Ruth.

"Stephen is strong. I was never any use to him. Just the one he protected."

"Someday," said Ruth, "you'll realize that needing a person is the greatest gift you can give him."

"I need all of you," I said. "Stay here. Help me. Let me help you. London killed my son. It's a city forsaken by God."

Stephen shook his head. "We have to go, Ruth and I. The Boar might follow her here. She hurt his pride as well as his skull and stole his crucifix."

John said: "I'm going to stay."

I packed them provisions of bread, beer, and salted bacon; gave them the Saracen poniard to use against thieves or sell in London; and strapped the rebec and kettledrums on their backs.

"You must have a livelihood in London," I said, when Stephen wanted to leave the instruments with John.

I walked with Stephen and Ruth to the wicket and gave them directions for finding the road: Walk a mile to the east ... look for the chestnut tree with a hole like a door in the trunk. . . .

But Stephen was looking over his shoulder for John.

"He stayed in the solar," I said. "He loves you too much to say good-bye."

"Or too little. Why else is he staying with you?"

"The world is a harsh place, Stephen. Harsher than the forest, and without any islands like the Manor of Roses." How could I make him understand that God had given me John in return for the son I had lost to the devil?

"I would be his island," said Stephen, his big frame shaken with sobs.

"Never mind," said Ruth. "Never mind. We'll come back for him, Stephen." And then to me: "My Lady, we thank you for your hospitality." She curtsied and kissed my hand with surprising warmth.

I said: "May an angel truly watch over you."

They marched toward the forest as proud and straight as Vikings, in spite of their wounds and their burdens. No more tears for Stephen. Not a backward look. London. Baghdad. Cathay!

It was then that I saw the face in the dense foliage, a bleached moon in a dusk of tangled ivy.

"Ruth, Stephen," I started to call. "You are being watched!"

But she had no eye for the children. She was watching me. I had seen her several times in the forest. Something of curiosity — no, of awe — distinguished her from the gray, anonymous tribe. Perhaps it was she who had left the crosses around my estate, like charms to affright the devil. She had never threatened

163

me. Once I had run from her. Like a wraith of mist before the onslaught of sunlight, she had wasted into the trees. I had paused and watched her with shame and pity.

Now, I walked toward her, compelled by a need which surpassed my fear. "I won't hurt you," I said. I was deathly afraid. Her friends could ooze from the trees and envelop me before I could cry for help. "I won't hurt you," I repeated. "I only want to talk."

The rank vegetable scent of her clogged my nostrils. I had always felt that the rose and the Mandrake represented the antitheses of the forest: grace and crookedness. Strange, though, now that I looked at her closely for the first time, she was like a crooked tree mistreated by many weathers; a natural object unanswerable to human concepts of beauty and ugliness.

Dredging archaic words from memories of old books, I spoke with soft emphasis. "Tell me," I said. "Why do you watch my house — my mead-hall? Is it treasure-rich to you? Broad-gabled?"

She caught my meaning at once. "Not mead-hall."

"What then? The roses perhaps? You may pick some if you like."

"Bantling."

"Bantling? *In my house?*"

She knelt and seized my hand and pressed her hairy lips against my knuckles.

"You," she said.

I flung my hands to my ears as if I had heard a

Mandrake shrief in the night. It was I who had shrieked. I fled . . . I fled. . . .

His eyes were closed, he rested against a cushion embroidered with children playing Hoodman Blind. He rose from his seat when he heard me enter the room.

"They're gone?"

"What? What did you say, John?"

"Stephen and Ruth are gone?"

"Yes."

He came toward me. "You're pale, Lady Mary. Don't be sad for me. I wanted to stay."

I said quietly: "I think you should go with your friends. They asked me to send you after them."

He blinked his eyes. The lids looked heavy and gray. "But I am staying to protect you. To be your son. You said —"

"It was really Stephen I wanted. You're only a little boy. Stephen is a young man. I would have taught him to be a gentleman and a knight. But now that he's gone, what do I need with a skinny child of twelve?"

"But I don't ask to be loved like Stephen!"

I caught him between my hands, and his lean, hard-muscled shoulders, the manhood stirring within him, belied my taunts.

"Go to him," I cried. "Now, John. You'll lose him if you wait!"

Pallor drained from his face, like pain routed by opium. "Lady Mary," he whispered. "I think I understand. You *do* love me, don't you? Enough to let me go. So much —"

I dropped my hands from his shoulders. I must not touch him. I must not kiss him. "So much. So much. . . ."

Beyond the hedge, he turned and waved to me, laughing, and ran to catch his friends. Before he could reach the woods, Stephen blazed from the trees.

"I waited," he cried. "I knew you would come!"

The boys embraced in such a swirl of color, of whirling bodies and clattering kettledrums, that the fair might have come to London Town! Then, arm in arm with Ruth, they entered the woods:

Summer is a-comin' in.
Loud sing cuckoo. . . .

I, also, entered the woods. For a long time I knelt before one of the stone crosses left by the Mandrakes — set like a bulwark between enormous oaks to thwart whatever of evil, griffins, wolves, men, might threaten my house. My knees sank through the moss to ache against stone; my lips were dry of prayer. I knelt, waiting.

I did not turn when the vegetable scent of her was a palpable touch. I said: "Would you like to live with me in the mead-hall?"

Her cry was human; anguish born of ecstasy. I might have said: "Would you like to see the Holy Grail?"

"Serve you?"

"Help me. You and your friends. Share with me."

I leaned to the shy, tentative fingers which loosened my hair and spread my tresses, as one spreads a fine brocade to admire its weave and the delicacy of its figures.

"Bantling," she said. "Madonna-beautiful." What had John said? "I love your hair when it's loose. It's like a halo. . . ." Roses and I have this in common: we have been judged too kindly by the softness of our petals.

"I must go now. Those in the mead-hall would not welcome you. I shall have to send them away. For your sake — and theirs. Tomorrow I will meet you here and take you back with me."

Earth, the mother of roses, has many children.

ACE
SCIENCE
FICTION
SPECIALS

10150 **Challenge The Hellmaker** Richmond $1.25	
20660 **Endless Voyage** Bradley $1.25	
21430 **Equality in the Year 2000** Reyndds $1.50	
25461 **From the Legend of Biel** Staton $1.50	
30420 **Growing Up In the Tier 3000** Gotschalk $1.25	
37171 **The Invincible** Lem $1.50	
46850 **Lady of the Bees** Swann $1.25	
66780 **A Plague of All Cowards** Barton $1.50	
71160 **Red Tide** Chapman & Tarzan $1.25	
81900 **Tournament of Thorns** Swann $1.50	

Available wherever paperbacks are sold or use this coupon.